# HARD WORKING MEN

## GAY EROTIC FICTION

EDITED BY
SHANE ALLISON

CLEIS
PRESS

Published in the United States by Cleis Press, Inc., 2246 Sixth Street, Berkeley, California 94710.

Cover design: Scott Idleman
Cover photograph: Jupiterimages
Text design: Frank Wiedemann
Cleis logo art: Juana Alicia
First Edition.
10 9 8 7 6 5 4 3 2 1

ISBN: 978-1-57344-406-4

"Digger" by Hank Edwards was previously published in *American Bear,* April/ May 2004 and *Bears: Gay Erotic Stories* (Cleis Press).

# HARD
# WORKING MEN

# Contents


vii    *Introduction: Men at Work*

1    *Lone Star Heat Wave* • ROB WOLFSHAM

16    *Body Shop* • AARON TRAVIS

29    *Blondie's Locks and the Three Bears* •
LOGAN ZACHARY

46    *Service Call* • MARVIN RICHMOND

60    *Unfinished Business* • DAVID SALCIDO

72    *Out on a Limb* • WILLIAM HOLDEN

89    *Summer Heat* • A. C. FARO

100    *Risky Sex* • BOB VICKERY

112    *Digger* • HANK EDWARDS

122    *Working the Weekend* • NEIL PLAKCY

131    *Frozen Stiff* • H. L. CHAMPA

144    *Back Room Buddies at the Rusty Screw* • JEFF FUNK

155    *The Hyphenated Handyman* • ROB ROSEN

165    *Cum-Slamming Handyman* • BEARMUFFIN

173    *Thresher* • ELAZARUS WILLS

188    *Black Caulk* • ZEKE MANGOLD

201    *A Married Construction Worker's Warm Mouth* •
SHANE ALLISON

207    *About the Authors*

211    *About the Editor*

# INTRODUCTION: MEN AT WORK

The doorbell startles me awake. I wipe the sleep from my eyes. I'm disoriented, not sure of the time of day. I look at the clock on my bedside table. It's a little after noon. I get out of bed and start toward the door. I shove my morning wood back through the slit of a cute pair of boxers with bananas printed on them.

When I open the door, the daylight burns my eyes. I squint with one eye open to make out the hunky form that stands on my doorstep. A white van that says CENTURY LINK CABLE on the side in big green letters is parked in front of my garage. He nearly towers over my measly five seven frame. Guy's gotta be at least six three, six four maybe. A small cardboard box is cocked beneath his arm. His smoke gray uniform is tight in all the right places. He looks like a male stripper. JORGE is embroidered in red on a patch of material that is sewn on the left side of his work shirt. He says good morning in a heavy, sexy Cuban accent. Latino guys are my favorite, preferably dressed in baggy jeans, a muscle T-shirt and tattoos like a second skin on muscle-bound arms. Jorge tells me he's here to fill a work order about hooking up my cable box. I barely remembered talking to them last week about sending someone out to hook it up.

My eyes start to get accustomed to the light. I invite him in so as not to be rude. I lead him to the TV that sits in an entertainment center in my living room. His tool belt bucks against a busty behind I want to smother my face in. Jorge pulls out the television and starts to tinker with black and white cables. My erection refuses to be still behind its tent of banana-printed boxers. I hold my hand over it, trying to keep it at bay with my fingers, but it's no use. Not when a hint of asscrack is exposed from the waist of Jorge's pants. I get ballsy and slowly slide my finger in. I feel his heat. It's electric. Surprisingly, Jorge doesn't object to my pass. He pulls himself from behind the TV to face me. I move my hand off my erection. It pokes out of the slit of my underwear. He smiles like he knows I was hard for him all along.

Jorge starts to run his hands across my chest: dirty, blue-collar fingers circle my nipples, causing further arousal. I press my hand against his crotch. He reaches under his tool belt and unzips. He reaches within the gape of his fly and pulls it out. I look at his piece that's bigger than I'd thought a dick could get. Jorge looks at me. I know what he wants. Precum is sticky and cold against my thigh. The carpet is soft under my knees. I take it and tip it up to my lips. Just when I'm about to do my business, I wake up.

It was a dream, another one of my sex dreams that reality yanks me out of just when things are about to get hot and heavy. I'm pissed and throw a pillow at a lamp that sits on my desk. I want to cry, knowing that I was that close to taste-testing that beefcake. I get up and take a leak, very horny from my wild dream. I sift through the stack of stories that now grace the pages of this anthology.

Here are just some of the treats ahead: Two construction

workers take their lusty lovemaking literally to new heights in veteran gay erotic scribe Bob Vickery's story, "Risky Sex." William Holden sets loins ablaze when a lonely neighbor gets a house call from a couple of hunky, horned-up tree trimmers in "Out on a Limb." Logan Zachary puts a new spin on a classic fairy tale when a sexy blond locksmith visits three brawny bears in "Blondie's Locks and the Three Bears." When a man living in wintry seclusion is paid a visit by a cable repairman in Marvin Richmond's "Service Call," things quickly start to heat up.

These seventeen hot tales get you inside the sweaty work clothes of a horny platoon of working dudes, from body shop owner to road worker, school custodian to thresher mechanic, HVAC repairman to arctic driller. Get ready for some strenuous on-the-job training.

Shane Allison
Tallahassee, Florida

# LONE STAR
# HEAT WAVE

Rob Wolfsham

Fucking August in Houston: ninety-four degrees, sixty percent humidity. I don't know what the heat index is from that—definitely over a hundred in my truck. Sweat and salt drip down my skin. I smack an itch on my neck as I drive. My truck smells like ripe ass and pipe grease. My toolbox kept slipping out of my hand so Jeff gave me a handle grip. I'll buy him a beer. The guys are in a good mood today because everyone's AC is clunking out on them. Calls are coming in like on a telethon. We do mostly commercial HVAC repair since we're a larger repair contractor. The smaller guys usually do houses, but we're getting loads of residential calls this week, too. The sky is not quite white from haze and ozone. The sun is an intense white glow from all around, diffused. If I had to name this blinding egg color, I'd call it bleak. I just finished sealing some leaky ducts at a Whole Foods Market, so it's been an easy day so far.

I walk into the rear office of Lone Star HVAC and Appliance

Repair Center and see Jones and Hernandez lounging next to the water cooler scraping wet paper towels across their sweaty foreheads.

"Forgot my sweater today," I say.

Hernandez grumbles and launches into how he had to install new compressors on three commercial units on top of the Target by the mall. He goes on and on. I slip my last work order in to be processed.

Rick, our squirrelly little boss with a mile-long goatee, slides me a residential job across the counter. It's in 77498, which is out in New Territory. "You'll need to haul ass," he says. "Their time was over thirty minutes ago."

"Why'd you wait for me to get back?" I whine.

"You see what I'm dealing with here?" Rick jerks his thumb at Hernandez and Jones, who look like they're melting in their gray button-up shirts.

"Hey, fuck you," Jones says. "I got heatstroke or something."

Rick leans over the counter on his elbows and says devilishly, "Look at Grant. Funny that the faggot is the only one not acting like a little bitch this week."

That shuts the guys up. I smile ear to ear with a peek of my tongue sticking out. We can joke like this. When the day is over we'll go to the Dam Ice House on Highway Six by the reservoir and get shit-faced. Rick will tell me about whatever sick shit he's done recently at nearby Asian spas while Jones, Hernandez and the others will drunkenly lament their bitchy wives and ungrateful kids and tell me that I'm lucky I get to fuck ass and get my dick sucked whenever I want.

The guys admire me. I'm a burly guy. I look grizzly. I keep my red beard and strawberry blond hair buzzed close. People think I'm military. I don't mind. I've got some tattoos from back when I was a moron in high school: barbed wires around my biceps, two coyotes on my forearms. On my chest I've got a sick skeleton *schutzstaffel* with red glowing eyes, an SS soldier. There used to be a swastika on the helmet. That was back when I was into being a skinhead and that stupid shit. I had it filled in when I moved on from that.

I haul my ass to New Territory, which is this wealthy suburb further west than Sugar Land. It takes about twenty minutes to get there through traffic. I get turned around in the maze of monotonous red-brick cookie-cutter mansions. Every house has two young oak trees planted in the front yard. Fake lakes and giant spewing fountains dot the neighborhood. The parks, biking paths and walking trails are empty. Physical activity isn't safe in this heat. Everyone is inside bitching about his air conditioner. *Ca-ching.*

I find my customer's house in a cul-de-sac the size of a small city block. The house dwarfs its neighbors with grand wings, a two-story portico and newly planted saplings scattered all over the football field of a front yard. I park my truck in front of the stone mailbox, not wanting to block two white GMC Yukons in the driveway.

A good-looking, familiar older guy answers the front door. His brown hair is slicked and combed over in that John Ritter-in-the-eighties sort of way. It has to be dyed because it shines even though he has the lined face of a man in his fifties. He looks like Jim Bob Duggar: round face, strong chin and pearly white teeth when he smiles. He's wearing a collared shirt with the sleeves rolled up, red and white stripes like a candy cane tucked into pressed khaki pants. He introduces himself as Jackson Tichy.

I recognize him. I've seen his beaming smile on the covers of books and billboards along highways. He's head of this huge megachurch in Houston. He notices the surprise in my face and relaxes, sighing, "Yes, I am Jack Tichy of Bristlepine Church. Thank you for making it out here today."

"I would have been here sooner," I say. "I had another call down at the Whole Foods Market."

"I can imagine," Jack says, face falling with faux concern for the working class. "It sure is sweltering. Please, come in."

He hesitates, holding a wry smile on me, taking a good look at the coyotes on my forearms.

"Grant Dunn," I say going for his hand. He shakes. "Of Lone Star H-V-A-C."

"Grant. Pleasure. Please come in, come in."

The foyer of his house has a pink marble floor and giant Christian-themed paintings along the stairway and below the balcony. My boot clicks echo off the high ceiling and crystal chandelier. It's hot in here, AC obviously out of commission or maybe shitty ducts and poor insulation. I can already tell it's one of those Trendmaker or KB Home mansions, where it looks nice but everything was built fast and cheap with ridiculous markup. This is why we have a housing crisis. And why he's probably having problems.

I look around like a kid in a museum. A giant painting of a young man being baptized in a river catches my attention. An old man is holding the kid's face underwater. It looks violent with white foamy splashing.

"Are you a congregant?" Jack asks.

"You mean in your church? Nope, I'm just a guy."

"Hey, that's okay," Jack says with saccharine enthusiasm. "We're all brothers. Grant, I'm going to ask you to take off your boots. My wife will go nuts if she sees them on the carpet."

I pause and look at my dirty black boots. I'm not wearing any socks. My feet are gonna fucking stink. The AC unit should be outside anyway, so I politely tell him this and he nods *of course.* He follows me outside and unlocks the back gate. There are two Trane AC units on the side of the house: one for the first floor, one for the second. One is roaring along, the other is idle.

We're both squinty under the white-hot sun. I get on my knees and tell Jack it'll take me a minute to assess the situation, which is code for leave me the fuck alone. Jack doesn't budge as I unscrew the maintenance cover from the idle unit. Being close to the grass makes it feel twice as humid on my face. Jack tries to make small talk about heat-related deaths on the news but praise Jesus his phone rings. He pulls out his BlackBerry and answers, wandering out the gate.

I see the problem with the AC: a shot condenser unit, a part for this model we don't have so it will have to be ordered. I run into Jack on the way to the front door. He looks hurried and suddenly irritated with me. "Grant, I'm afraid I gotta run. Sorry about that. You *were* a little late."

"It's okay. I figured out part of the problem, but I need to look at your ducts."

Jack glances at his watch, then at the house, looking toward the second floor. "My son is home." He bites his lip. "I'd hate to reschedule on you." His saccharine smile returns. "Do what you need to do. Just remember, take off your shoes."

He prances to one of the parked GMC Yukons and says, "Let my son know you're here so he doesn't get scared."

He drives off in an unchristian manner. What a nagging bitch. He sounded a little fey when he got flustered. He's gotta be your typical Ted Haggard or some shit like that, snorting coke off twink prostitute ass at South Beach on the weekends, then having angry frustrating sex with his wife until he's just frantically flapping over her vagina with his eyes closed.

I walk into the house and keep my boots on. The dining room connects to the foyer. A family portrait sits above the long pine table, bounded on both sides by two giant wood crucifixes. Jack looks forlorn and heavy, looking off in the distance with a thousand-yard stare. His chubby wife has explosive blonde hair cascading over her red business suit shoulder pads. Their son is smiling brightly with braces and a suit like his father's. He looks about sixteen with bright sky-colored eyes and brown shaggy hair. Not a bad-looking kid. I wonder how long ago this was taken.

I'm guessing the son is upstairs since the house is quiet. I head up there to see the ductwork, passing by several hutches with fine china that has Jesus and thorns and apostles on them, like the kind of shit you'd only see on a three a.m. infomercial on the fishing channel. I'm tainting this white pristine house, the white carpets, the white walls and glowing religious-themed paintings of goats and bearded men looking at deserts.

I smell like grass and armpit. I fluff my Lone Star HVAC shirt fanning hot air off my chest, skeleton soldier breathing. I stomp up the stairs and the house gets more silent, a water pipe shutting off.

At the top of the stairs is a walkway over the den that splits into two hallways. A door opens on the left hallway. A teenage boy walks out wrapped in a towel, dripping wet. His dark hair is longer, down to his neck. He's got a smooth runner's build, much older looking than the photo, tall, more defined like a man. He notices me frozen on the catwalk staring at him. Our eyes catch and he darts into a room across the hall, delicately closing the door.

I feel a pang of awkwardness and realize it's just me getting a boner. "I'm the AC repair guy," I say loudly into the hallway. "I'll be in the attic."

I barely hear him say, "Gotcha."

I find the attic stairs and discover it's 120 degrees up there. I explore the maze of aluminum ducts in the darkness for a few minutes. I'm raining sweat. My feet are sopping around in my boots. I should have worn socks. I growl and stick a small flashlight between my teeth and unbutton my shirt. The insulation is a disaster and the main line is separating from the intake. This will be a big job. I can't take the heat anymore and head back to the second floor.

I fold up the attic stairs and when I look down from the door, the boy is standing a few feet in front of me. He's still wrapped in his towel even though he's dry. My hairy chest is gleaming with sweat, and my tattoo of the red-eyed skeleton soldier is staring at this kid. He stares back at the grinning skull on my chest. My crotch feels wet.

He inspects me and says, "Are you going to fix it? A shower was the only way I could cool off."

I wipe my face with one side of my shirt. It doesn't really help. The kid sounds gay; I'm talkin' lisping, soft spoken, shy. My eyes roam his body. He's tan, thin. His stomach looks strong, no happy trail. The veins in his arms stick out.

I scratch the sticky nest of hair on my chest. He doesn't seem bothered that I'm a stranger standing here, shirt unbuttoned. "I think so," I say. "But I got a lot to do."

"Will it be like today?" he asks. His eyes dart to my crotch, the movement almost obscured by two quick blinks.

"If we can get the parts from another supplier in the city. How old are you?"

"Eighteen."

"I'm Grant," I say.

"Stephen." I realize he lisps a little because he still has braces. They're kind of a turn-on, like vulnerability.

I'm crumbling with lust, but I feign confidence, raising my chin, letting my shirt come farther apart around my sides. I don't have cliché abs, but guys like the brawny definition I do have, you know, muscles I actually use, not just show. I hate that I'm a pasty white fucker, but I just burn if I try to tan. Fuck my redhead genes. I'm doing this tough-guy shit for him to mask the quaking in my thighs and calves. This boy is what I want. Shaggy brown hair covers his left eye like the emo boys I like to pick up at Numbers and fuck the shit out of. Except this boy is pure, no tattoos, no piercings. My boner is screaming against my briefs.

"So you took a shower?" It's obvious my mind is spinning on the image. "That sounds nice."

"You look like you're dying," he says. "Maybe you should take one, too."

I'm knocked back for a second. I literally take a step back. This kid is evil. I like it. The rubber grip for my toolbox gets so sweaty it slips from my hand and the whole thing crashes to the carpet, tools exploding everywhere.

I bend down and growl, scooping up bits. I'm supposed to be smooth. This boy has me tripped up. This boy knows what he's doing. Or maybe it's a Christian naivete, unintentionally covering up some subconscious pull to get me naked, his id screaming for cock.

"Offer hospitality to one another without grumbling," he says matter-of-factly, watching me scoop tools off the carpet.

"What?"

"It's from Peter. My dad says it a lot."

"Oh, the Bible." I stand, huffing.

"Are you a Christian?" he asks, scanning the evil-looking tattoo on my chest and the rabid coyotes on my arms.

I think about ripping this kid's towel off and raping his ass right here on the carpet. "No."

"Do you at least have faith in something?" he asks in that tip-of-the-iceberg way.

"I worship Satan."

His head turns askance a little, smooth pink lips curled with uncertainty, revealing a peek of his braces as he scans my evil tattoos again. He smirks. "Joking right?"

"Yeah, c'mon. But I am an atheist."

He smiles with that *let me take you in* love and starts to extol the strength of his father and the strength Jesus gives him and the strength the Bible imparts and the strength of my abs thrusting dick in his ass. My brain threw in that last part, because the boy is in a fucking towel and I'm a sweaty hormonal monkey and I'm not really listening to him. But I let him go on about his God thing. I discover the paper-thin line between Baptist witnessing and faggotry. Someone has to stop the Jesus-go-round so I remind him about the shower.

"I know it's probably weird, but that would be nice," I say.

"Of course, brother. The bathroom is down here," he says, leading me down the hall.

*Brother.* Kinky.

The bathroom is the size of my living room with a glass shower and a Jacuzzi tub in front of a large Monticello window facing the backyard with a view of one of those fake lakes with an ejaculating fountain. The room is steamy like a solarium or greenhouse because it's on the north side of the house, facing the summer afternoon sun.

I ignore the shower and start filling the tub. I strip to nothing. Stephen doesn't move. I turn around and sit on the rim of the Jacuzzi facing him, legs spread. My seven-inch boner stands tall. It's a fine redhead boner, pearly white pole, bright pink head. My fire crotch fans up my navel and loosely defined abs into a hairy *T* crossing over my skeleton soldier tattoo and my pecs. I grip the sides of the tub beside me, coyotes on my forearms staring at the boy. I lean back a little, shrugging as the tub fills and gurgles.

He has a look of biblical consternation, crusade and martyrdom glistening through two blue eyes. His Adam's apple moves like he would say something, but he bolts out the bathroom door.

Smooth Grant. Maybe I misread him, treated this too much like I was going to bang an eager skater punk or emo boy from the club. Those guys know what they want as much as I do. Stephen has a few more ancient variables.

The tub thrashes with luke-cool water and I sink in to my chin. Muscles unwind. I stroke my dick thinking of Stephen's smooth navel and likely smooth ass bouncing on my balls. How absurd is it—the HVAC specialist taking a bath in a client's house, Jack Tichy's house no less, and exposing himself to the pastor's eighteen-year-old son?

Several minutes pass and the door cracks open, a phone held in a hand peeking through the opening.

"Your phone is ringing," Stephen says meekly. It must have come off my belt clip when I was picking up my tools.

"Bring it," I command.

There's no movement for a few seconds. Then he enters looking at the ceiling, holding the phone out. He's wearing track pants, no shirt. Sunlight through the window makes his tan skin glow. The phone is no longer vibrating. It takes me a few seconds to scoot to the edge of the tub toward him. I take the phone and it says I have one missed call from Rick. I lay it on the side of the tub.

"Feels great," I say. "You must be spoiled by this."

He says nothing and starts to walk out.

Impatience surges through my spine. "Wait."

"Don't take too long. My dad will be home."

I say nothing for a few seconds, mind rushing like the jets of water around my back. I scoot back in the tub. "Get in."

He takes an eternity to think. I almost say something again but he peels off his track pants. He has a pasty ass with a fading tan line at his hips. He turns around: dark bush, large flaccid cock, dangling balls. His skinny legs climb into the tub. There's enough room in this tub for four grown men. I spread my feet. He swims to my chest, hugging me, curling under my neck. He's shaking like he's freezing.

My hands scratch his ribs. Then my fingertips run down his vertebrae. He twists against me, arms shivering harder. I put my lips on his hair, not quite kissing, just mouthing. His dick hardens against my hairy taint until it prods at my asshole with each one of his twists. I haven't bottomed in years. I'm a take-charge guy, but right now I'd let this boy discover ass, what evils lie inside.

I swing around him and grab his asscheeks, lifting his crotch out of the water. He's blessed with a large tool, seven inches and thick, larger than mine, which makes me feel funny for a second. I take in his gift, swallowing it down. He hyperventilates, unprepared for the feeling of chin stubble grinding his balls. He loses his grip in the tub and slips underwater. I grab his shoulders and yank him back up. He's coughing and spitting water. I laugh. My first baptism.

He jolts from my grip and jumps out of the tub. I think that's the end of it, but he kicks his bunched-up track pants aside and grabs a bunch of towels off the racks and throws them on the checkered tiles. He lies down, spreading his legs; then he's perfectly still, holding his arms straight at his sides, fists clenched. His dick bobs a little, straining at the upper limit of an erection. I jump out of the tub and climb over him, water slopping off of me. Beads of water cover his chest, which rises and falls each second. Water drips off me onto him. He looks straight up at the ceiling and doesn't blink.

I press my face low to the floor between his thighs, rubbing against the towel until my nose digs under his balls and lifts them up. I get a fresh soapy smell and a tone of ass musk. He's got a fuzz of black hair around the rim of his asscheeks. I lick his bacon strip from his ass up to his balls, long and sloppy, a big long dog lick, diving back down to tickle his hole with my tongue. He groans and lifts his ass off the towel. I spread his cheeks with my thumbs and get a look at his pink hole. I dive back in, jamming my tongue in him.

"What. What are you doing," he moans. I don't think he expected this. I don't think he even knew someone would do this to him. I chuckle into his ass and get my whole tongue through the tight ring of his sphincter and fuck him with it. I grab his dick and a glob of precum oozes over my fingers like a lava flow. I jack him and replace my tongue with a thumb, slipping it easily into his saliva-drenched hole.

He clenches the towel in his fists and tilts his head back, arching off the floor. He squirms from side to side, wet hair tossing over one eye. I put my lips on the head of his cock and swirl my tongue around as I jack him and shove my thumb in his ass to the base. We in the HVAC specialist business call this giving someone the works. Of course that's referring to ventilation systems, not eighteen-year-old boys.

Stephen lets out a whimpering groan, chest arching up, relaxing, arching up again like a writhing little bitch. I jack and suck the Jesus out of him, pounding my lips against my fist jacking his cock. I tilt my right thumb back, pushing his prostate up. I don't think he's going to last much longer as I feel his sphincter pulse around my knuckle. His breathing goes spastic and he pounds the floor with his fists still clenching towel. Cum splatters against my lips just as I'm pulling outward to suckle the head. I dive down again, jacking him furiously, licking his frenulum. Cum fills my mouth and I swallow it down since I know he's an untouched thing.

I pump and suck him dry and pull my thumb out gently savoring the nice pinch of his tight ass. I stroke his balls gently like a chin. He has tears in his eyes, still not looking at me. I feel like a rapist for a second but he makes a hint of a smile, braces glistening.

A home security panel on the wall beeps twice indicating the front door has just opened.

Stephen's smile vanishes and he darts to his feet, snatching up his track pants. "You can't be in here," he barks under his breath.

Well, fuck.

"Stephen?" a Texan voice calls from the stairs. It's his father, Jackson Tichy. "Stephen, is that repair guy still here?"

Stephen runs past the tub and unlatches the Monticello window. It opens out like a door.

"Are you fucking kidding me?" I grumble and slide on my jeans, forcing my boner down before zipping up.

"I'm sorry," Stephen whispers, hushing me.

There's a knock on the door and the boy's tan disappears. "Stephen, are you in here?"

Fuck! I look out the window and see an unforgiving red-brick façade all the way down about thirty feet to the grass. There's an oak tree but it's too far and too young. There are small ledges and footholds where the bricks form stylized trimmings.

There's no time. I climb out backward in just my jeans, hanging on to the edge of the window. My bare feet touch a hot brick ledge below. It's only about five inches wide. The thought of falling and breaking my neck crosses my mind, and I think about climbing back into the bathroom to face Jack Tichy. I have no reason to fear him. What's the most he could do? Well, I guess accuse me of raping his son. He's rich and famous enough to legally smote me and probably Lone Star HVAC, too. Or would he even think that? Could I just say, *Oh, I've been climbing out here all along, looking at ventilation ducts or something? I always climb up to the second floor of houses without a ladder or safety equipment. We don't have to worry about union rules in Texas. Sure. Why am I not wearing a shirt? Or shoes? Because I'm a wild nature man who needs cheap thrills in his life. Kind of like sucking your son's dick.*

Something whooshes over my head. My boots. Then my shirt. Then my toolbox. I cringe. The tools crash on the grass far below with one loud crunch. I hear the bathroom door open and Jack says, "Why are you taking a bath in the middle of the day?"

"Dad, everything is fine. I was hot, okay?"

I worry about Stephen for a second, but now I'm actually pissed, pissed enough that I climb down to the top ledge of a first floor window. I eventually make it to the grass after a few trembling minutes, motivated by the thought of Jack coming outside and seeing me like this.

On the ground, I pull my gray Lone Star HVAC uniform shirt down from a low tree branch and frantically put it on and button it up. I shove my feet into my boots. I scrape tools into my toolbox along with clumps of grass.

Jack Tichy comes around the corner of the house, power walking like a homo. My heart leaps at the sight of him barging toward me. I stand up straight.

"There you are," he says. "I'm glad I was able to come back. I wanted to touch base with you before you left."

He stops and stares at me like I'm missing an arm. My shirt has leaves stuck in it. My jeans are covered in grass stains. I wipe my lips, paranoid there might be leftover cum from his son.

"You're soaking wet!" he cries.

I nod.

His face twists with genuine concern for the working class. "Grant, you look like you're having a heatstroke. Please come inside. Have a glass of water."

He starts walking and I follow, a jumble of words caught in my throat, something between "Sure," and "Thank you."

He looks back at me, scanning my disheveled, tired, still horny body. His eyes narrow with something more than concern, some curious conflicting possibility. "Maybe you should take a shower, too."

# BODY SHOP

Aaron Travis

Hey, Boss." Smitty stops cold on his way out of my office, staring through the blinds of the big picture window onto the street below. From the smartass expression on his face, I can tell what's coming. "It's the kid again." Smitty gives me a sidelong smirk. I smirk back.

Hell, Smitty knows what's going on between me and Cory. So what? I'm the boss around this place. Besides, despite the wife and the rug rats he's got hanging around his neck, I wouldn't be surprised if Smitty isn't more than a little bit jealous.

I get up and walk over to the window. Sure enough, there's Cory, standing across the street. Not really standing: he can't keep still for two seconds. He paces back and forth, leans his hip against the mailbox for a second, pushes himself away and slaps his hand against the telephone pole, crosses his arms and gives the pole a kick, spins around and paces some more. All the while he keeps glancing up at the window, unable to see past the blinds.

"Looks like he needs something," says Smitty, "bad." Shit, even Smitty's getting off looking at him, wearing a sneer on his face like a fox who's found the chicken coop door wide open. But this bird is mine.

Cory is very short and very wide. They say kids start lifting weights in the first grade these days; I'll bet Cory started in preschool. How else could a nineteen-year-old have a body like that? Big square shoulders and a muscle-padded chest tapering down to hardly any waist at all, then blossoming out into an oversized backside that could split the seams of most jeans wide open. He's got wavy jet black hair on his head and nowhere else, except for a few wisps under his arms and a tiny patch between his legs. Smooth and sleek all over, like a big lollipop. He keeps looking up at the window, biting his lip and drawing his eyebrows together. He's got the kind of face that makes teenage girls wet their panties, and he's never looked better than he looks right now, fretting and nervous and totally unsure of himself.

Today he must need it real bad. If he walked all the way from his dorm room to the body shop dressed like that, I'm surprised he hasn't gotten his butt plugged already—this is the kind of outfit that gets rape cases thrown out of court. White Reeboks and white socks. Sleek brown thighs so muscled up they slip and slide against each other when he walks. A snap-tight spaghetti-strap yellow tank top that shows off his dark tan and his big bouncy pecs—as he turns and paces I keep catching glimpses of nipple.

In between the socks and the tank he's legally dressed, but just barely. The black shorts look like spandex, but they're definitely not cycling shorts. In front they're slung low enough to leave a gap that shows two inches of midriff below his navel. Farther down the stuff clings to his box and pushes it out between his naked thighs. In back it clings tighter than skintight to his ass and rides so high it shows off almost as much cheek as thigh.

The kid looks obscene.

My mouth starts watering. It's time for Smitty to get lost. I give him an elbow in the ribs and he jumps—he staring as hard as I am. "Get outta here, you dirty old man," I tell him, but if twenty-nine is old what does that make me at thirty-five? Shit, I've had a dirty mind since I sprang my first hard-on drooling over the underwear ads. Cory probably started whacking off watching music videos about the same time he started pumping iron.

"Go on," I tell Smitty, "get your ugly ass outta here. Find something to do down in the shop. And make sure the guys all stay busy for the next hour or so. And if some stupid customer comes around here with a problem, you handle it. No fucking phone calls, either!"

Smitty backs out of the office but not without flashing me that shit-eating smirk one more time. Just as he's closing the door he very distinctly mouths the word "Assfucker." I pick up a brass paperweight from the desk and put another big dent in the door. After the crash I hear Smitty snickering outside. Shit, he just wishes it was him getting into the kid's pants. I turn back to the window, raise the blinds and look out. Cory looks up and spots me. For just a second I catch my own reflection in the glass. I'm wearing the same smartass smirk that Smitty's always flashing.

Cory's nervous. I can see his Adam's apple bob even from this far away. He makes a motion to stuff his hands in his pockets, except that he hasn't got any—no room for pockets in those skimpy little shorts. Instead he ends up nervously stroking the tops of his thighs, and maybe not even knowing it he reaches between his legs with one hand and presses at his crotch. He just stares up at me. He's afraid to come into the body shop. He knows the guys'll snicker at him and make noises behind his back.

It all started about six weeks ago. Cory brought in the little red Corvette his daddy had given him for high school graduation. The front end looked like maybe Godzilla had stepped on it. He'd accidentally run a red light and slammed the side of a UPS van. Nobody was hurt and Daddy's insurance covered everything. Cory was a bigger mess than the 'Vette—shaken up, embarrassed, worried, feeling like a stupid jerk. I could see right off that he was the type of kid who doesn't know shit about cars and feels like a real dumbass in a body shop.

I should've been nice but I wasn't. Looking at his big doe eyes and his trembling upper lip and his big muscles all over, I just couldn't help myself. I got a hard-on, and when I get a hard-on the rest of me does what it says. I double-talked him, fast-talked him and generally put on my best sleazy con-artist routine just for the fun of watching him squirm. What I really wanted was to watch him squirm out of his twenty-seven-inch jeans and into my lap.

I took him up to the office, supposedly to finish some paperwork. Shit, the paperwork was already done. What I had in mind was working on Cory.

Laying him was almost too easy. All I had to do was step into the john for a minute and leave the door open, talking all the time like it was the most natural thing in the world. I hauled out my eight semisoft inches and took a long hard piss. Toward the end of it I looked up at the mirror and caught Cory staring at my back like he was gearing up for Mr. Teen America and I was his next steroid injection.

I took the hunch. I shook my dick and then turned around and casually walked up to him, sort of like I'd just forgotten to stuff all that dangling meat back into my pants. I could feel my cock sway and thicken in front of me and my balls slap back against the bottom seam of my jeans. Cory stared at my crotch slack-jawed and backed against the wall, like I had a king cobra between my legs bobbing its head and ready to strike.

It didn't take much encouragement to get him to touch it. After that it was a piece of cake to talk him into kissing it. And once he'd felt it on his lips he naturally wanted it in his mouth. Cory was born to suck cock.

I came all over his face. He came all over the floor. Afterward, I pitched him a greasy rag from my desk and told him to clean up the mess. He got down on his hands and knees like a scrub maid, with his pants still down around his ankles. I walked around and got my first look at his butt. Jesus! I was hard as a rock again in two seconds flat. Then the phone started ringing, somebody started banging at the door, and Smitty was calling me on the intercom. I took a deep breath and promised myself: *Later*.

And sure enough, a few days later Cory dropped in again, "Just to see how things are going." The 'Vette was coming along fine, but Cory needed another fix of dick. In fifteen minutes I had him bent over my desk, sweaty and naked with ten solid inches of rubber-skinned cock up his cherry-busted ass. He whined and whimpered so loud I figured they had to be able to hear him down in the shop. He left the place bowlegged and limping, with a funny grin on his face.

The next time I saw him was when he dropped by to pick up the car. Daddy came along too, just to make sure nobody got screwed, so to speak. My cock was like a lead pipe straining against my pants leg, trying to figure a way into Cory's butt. I'd pretty much given up on the proposition when Cory suggested he take the car for a spin around the block just to make sure the engine sounded smooth, with me in the front seat to answer any questions. Cory's dad stayed behind; Cory's dad was not the sort of man to ride in the luggage seat of a red Corvette.

Once we were out of sight, Cory pulled over and we changed places. I tooled around the city for half an hour while his throat did a hungry number on my stick shift. Have you ever gotten off doing ninety down a city expressway with a cock-starved nineteen-year-old between your legs? If the opportunity should ever present itself, don't think twice.

After that, Cory started dropping by maybe twice a week. I'm not shy, and the guys who work for me aren't stupid. They caught on to what was happening pretty quick. Cory was definitely not brought up to play a boss mechanic's private grease monkey in front of an audience, but what he craves, he craves, and he doesn't seem able to resist. Which makes it more and more interesting every time he drops by.

This time I decide to make him wait. I settle down behind my desk, prop my feet up and light a stogie. There's a buddy I need to talk to about a poker game Thursday night. I reach for the phone. He's not in, but I blow five minutes bullshitting with his secretary. She's been putting the make on me for ten years with no luck.

I take a final puff and snuff out the cigar. A quick check at the window: Cory's still there, staring up like a hound dog at the moon. I'd make him wait longer, but my balls are starting to ache.

I step out the door and skip down the metal spiral stairs. Smitty spots me and smirks, but nobody else knows what's up. I cross the pools of grease on the floor, step out into the sunlight and saunter across the street.

Cory waits by the mailbox, kicking out his feet, flicking his eyes back and forth from my crotch to the sidewalk. I walk up, lean against the telephone pole, shake my head and whistle real low. "You look like a ten-dollar whore."

It's not quite what he was expecting. Cory blushes and bites his lip. He gets all shifty eyed. I can see he's thinking about flying the coop. No way.

I edge a little closer and cup his ass. The palm of my hand is against the spandex. My fingers are against the naked bottom curve of his cheek—skin like warm silk. Cory grabs the sides of the mailbox, like he needs the support. He draws back his lips; I can see the tip of his tongue between his teeth. I slip my middle finger under the hem of his shorts and into his crack.

I find his pucker and start playing with it—poking at it, stroking it, snapping my fingernail against it. He gives a gasp and loosens up right away. I press my fingertip against the opening, meaning to push in to the first knuckle—and my whole finger slides all the way in.

"You always go out of the house with your hole greased up?" I twist my finger inside him. He narrows his eyes and grunts.

"Huh? What, you want to be ready for the first dick that comes along? Or do you save it for the really big ones?" Deep inside I can feel his prostate against my fingertip, all plump and swollen, needing to be pumped and emptied real bad. He's probably got a pint of juice inside him that needs to get out. "Or maybe you just grease it up on the days you go out wearing your tight little fuck-me shorts. Hmm?"

I can actually feel him blush around my finger—I'd know he was blushing even in the dark. His hole clamps down, just the way he bites down on his lower lip, and inside I can feel a vein begin to pulse alongside my finger. I start stroking in and out. He's like cream velvet inside, hot and slick and smooth.

"Come on. Let's get into my office."

He steps forward and then stiffens when he realizes that I

intend to keep my finger up his butt while we cross the street. He gets a look on his face like he's just swallowed something by accident and he's not sure what it was.

"Come on. Move your ass." I grab his hand and brush it against the bulge at my groin. His fingers linger on the lump, then snap away as a truck turns onto the street and passes us. He walks forward as fast as he can, with a groan and an awkward little limp. I keep wriggling my finger in his hole, stirring his insides.

Once we're in the shop I pull my finger out, but I make sure his shorts stay pulled way up into the crack of his ass. I walk ahead of him and trot up the stairs. He walks behind, but I can see him in my mind's eye: hands at his sides, his face bowed, his shoulders rigid. A couple of the guys make noises and whistle; Smitty probably spread the word the second I stepped outside. When I close the office door behind us the kid lets out a long hard sigh.

"Your outfit's a big hit," I tell him. He lowers his head and moves his arms around like he's trying to cover himself. I put my hand on his neck and walk him over to the desk. I slide my hand from his neck down his spine to the small of his back and onto the curve of his ass.

"Cute panties," I say. He groans and blushes an even deeper shade of red. "Take 'em off."

They're so tight he has to roll them over the hard high muscles of his ass and down his thighs. Once they're over his knees they flutter down to his ankles and he steps out of them, raising his legs like a show pony.

Now he's wearing nothing but white socks and sneakers and a tank top so small it won't cover both nipples. I can't help but let out a low whistle; the kid's got an ass that could stop traffic. It made my heart skip a beat the first time I saw it, and it's done the same thing every time since. Hard and round, sleek and shiny: if he had a tattoo that read FUCK ME it couldn't be more inviting.

"Pull your cheeks apart." He reaches back and grabs two fistfuls of sleek ass. "That's it, spread that crack wide open for me. Bend over and give me a look."

Is there anything as pretty as a muscleboy's virgin fuckhole? Damn, as far as I know he hasn't found anybody else to fuck it except me. Unlikely, but possible. Maybe he's too scared to come on to his frat brothers.

I stroke the crack with the edge of my hand, then slip two fingers inside, wriggling them back and forth as if I were tickling him. He gasps out loud. "Let go of your cheeks," I tell him. "Grab your ankles." I want to feel the sweaty inside of his cheeks against both sides of my hands while I finger-fuck him.

He starts groaning. I reach between his big smooth thighs, find his cock and pull it backward. Not a big cock but damned pretty, tightly circumcised, smooth and sleek and elegantly shaped, just like his little red Corvette. I pinch the plump head between my thumb and forefinger while I goose him good, finger-fucking him just a little too fast and a little too hard, until his sloppy hole is farting air and he's making a funny whimper deep in his throat. His cock is hard as rubber and leaking on the floor. I let go and listen to it slap against his hard belly.

I keep a finger up his hole while I unbutton my jeans and circle around. I put a hand in his hair and pull his head up as far as it'll go with his fists around his ankles. I rub his face in my crotch. He mumbles and slobbers and I feel a hot wet tongue all over my cock and balls and burrowing underneath. Cory is a funky kid. Cory has a sloppy mouth. One of these days I'm going to keep him in the office for a whole afternoon, just prop my legs up wide apart and let him go to town lapping and scrubbing and burying his face between my legs, getting every inch of me hot and wet and sloppy from the inside ring of my asshole to the leaky tip of my dick.

I let go of his hair and reach for the foil packet by the ashtray. I tear it open with my teeth and pull out the rubber. I start sliding it over the crown—hard to do one-handed with a cock that big—and he lets go of his ankles, staying low and reaching for it. "Let me!" he gasps, and his eyes go all milky and unfocused. I keep stirring my fingers up his asshole while he reverently rolls the rubber down over my shaft. It's like a holy rite. He's bent over with his face close to it, looking like a choirboy in ecstasy, his hands cupped together like he's praying.

"Good enough," I tell him. "Grab your ankles again." I pull my fingers out of him with a pop and line up behind him, dipping my cock toward the greasy, sweaty crack of his ass. I pull his cheeks apart. His hole shrinks away for a second, and then it puffs out, opening up like a flower, like the moist pink lips are straining out to give the head of my cock a sloppy kiss.

I give him just the head to start with. He always has a hard time taking it at first, no matter how much I've loosened him up. I like hearing him moan. When the moans die down a little, I make him moan some more by slipping him another inch or two. By the time I'm all the way in he's shaking like a leaf and lathered with sweat, like a racehorse after a hard run. I can hear it dripping off him onto the grimy linoleum floor.

I start pumping. Cory throws his head this way and that and grinds his ass back into my hips. Then I start pumping harder, hard enough that he has to let go of his ankles and grab the desktop. I run my hands all over his hot, slick ass, up the flaring muscles of his back, underneath to grab his big meaty pecs, popping his nipples between my forefingers and thumbs.

Cory's gasping, grunting. "Fuck me! Fuck me!"

I bring my arms up, turning the tank top inside out and pushing it over his head. He straightens up a little. Then I pull the tank back toward me, bringing his arms with it, pulling them into a cross behind his back, wrapping the little scrap of sweat-soaked cloth around his wrists, holding it tight like a rein. Then we go for a ride.

I cock-walk him around the room, pushing him forward with my knees, steering him with my cock deep in his guts, giving his ass an occasional slap with my free hand, till one cheek is cherry red and the other's milky white. He staggers and trips—a dick up his ass makes him into a spastic. Damn, I'd like to walk him down the street this way—walk him across campus so all his buddies could have a good look at Cory shamefaced and naked getting his butt screwed. Maybe he'd even like it, getting a chance to show off the thing he does best.

I walk him face-first into the wall. He hardly seems to notice. I swing him around and scoot him into the middle of the room with a series of quick, deep jabs. He's starting to get really noisy. I know they can hear him down in the shop.

And then I start walking him toward the door, toward the keyhole, step by step, screwing him hard and deep, making him put on a good show. Because something tells me...

It takes only a second to swing around and grab the doorknob, unlock the button with my thumb and jerk it open. Smitty's pressed so hard against the keyhole he actually tumbles into the room.

Cory goes stiff and his sphincter clamps down like a vise. He tries to pull away, but I won't let him, holding tight to his tangled-up wrists. Smitty looks up at me and for the first time in his life there's not even the hint of a smirk on his face. His eyes are like half-dollars and his mouth is all screwed up. It's hard not to laugh. Almost as hard as it is not to start shooting up Cory's butt at that very instant.

"You sneaky son of a bitch," I growl, slamming the door shut with my foot. For just a second, I really feel angry. I knock the cap off Smitty's head and grab a fistful of his greasy black hair. And the next thing I know Smitty's face is buried in the kid's crotch, and I'm holding it there. Or am I? It almost seems like Smitty went for Cory's dick and my hand just followed along. All I know is, it doesn't take any effort at all to keep him there.

Cory doesn't seem to mind. His ass starts doing stuff it's never done before, swallowing my dick the way Smitty's swallowing his. I manage to drive home a few hard lunges, and then it's happening. Cory's ass squeezes like a fist, matching me pump for pump while I start unloading. Down below I hear Smitty gagging and choking, spewing the kid's come in a warm spray against my naked balls.

When it's over I stagger back, pop free of Cory's hole, peel off the rubber and toss it in the corner. I flop back into the tattered easy chair and try to keep my eyes open while Cory hops around the room like a scared rabbit, squeezing back into his tank top and shorts and clearing out of the room in fifteen seconds flat.

Smitty's still on his knees, blinking his eyes. There's come dripping from his chin. He didn't even have time to get his dick out.

Now I'm really mad. "Smitty, you peeping-tom son of a bitch. You've scared him off. Best damned piece of ass…"

"Don't worry, Boss. He'll be back." Smitty wipes his mouth with the back of his hand.

"Oh, yeah? One look at your ugly mug—"

"Hey, it's not like him and me hadn't done it before." He bites his lip, like he's said something he didn't mean to.

It takes a second for the words to register. "Smitty, what the hell are you talking about?"

He looks shamefaced, but I can see the smirk lurking at the corner of his mouth. "Hell, Boss, you know last Thursday, when you was down at that meeting all day? Well, the kid dropped by, horny as a goat, you know how he gets, and since you weren't here—"

"Smitty, you lousy—"

"Now wait, I never trespassed on your territory. We just did—well, what we did today. I guess you could say I'm what they call oral-fixated."

And suddenly I realize he's staring hard at my dick, drooping naked and half-hard from the fly of my jeans.

"Anyway, the kid says you're always good for at least two rounds." Smitty licks his lips.

"Smitty, you grease-monkey son of a bitch." I feel a surge of blood into my dick, and all of a sudden the room goes dim. "Reach up and lock that door behind you. Good. Now crawl over here on your hands and knees. Let's see if I can't wipe that smirk off your face once and for all."

# BLONDIE'S LOCKS AND THE THREE BEARS

**Logan Zachary**

B londie's Locks, where everything is locked up tight. Blondie speaking."

"Do you offer twenty-four-hour service?" a husky male voice asked.

"I'm the sole owner and employee of Blondie's Locks, so if I'm free, I'm willing to do what I can, but it all depends on my schedule."

"This is Thomas Vasquez. I live in the gay ghetto, and we had a few break-ins last night. I'm calling for myself and the three bears in the neighborhood."

Blondie laughed.

"No, I'm serious. Everyone calls them the three bears. They are the three Kodiak brothers, and they're my neighbors. I thought you would've heard of them."

"Sorry, I thought you were pulling my leg."

"Anyway, we need new locks on all our homes."

"Is there a reason the brothers aren't calling me themselves?"

"It's Saturday, and they work weekends."

"That's nice that you're helping them out."

"We do what we can to help each other out. Besides, I'm sure you'd rather have one call instead of four."

"True. So, how do I get into their homes to replace their locks?"

"Oh, they'll be home. Trust me, they work from their houses." He quickly gave him the addresses and hung up.

Blondie wondered as he packed up his supplies, what business could be so busy that they couldn't call for service? He would soon find out.

The whole house thumped with *Dirty Deeds Done Dirt Cheap* as Blondie rang the doorbell. Several seconds later, Pat Kodiak answered the door in a leather vest and chaps. A red studded leather jock covered his manhood and framed his ass to perfection. His body glistened with sweat and the scent of hard work and sex. His leather clung to his body like a second skin.

"I'm here about the locks," Blondie shouted over the music.

A young man's naked body hung in a sling suspended from the ceiling. His legs were spread wide open, welcoming. His hard-on stood straight up. Several dildos and butt plugs were lined up on a table like surgical instruments. A pool of lube puddled below him.

"If this is a bad time..."

"We don't mind if you don't mind," Pat said.

The young man's head popped up to see who was at the door; a red ball gag filled his mouth.

"You don't mind if he works on the locks?" Pat shouted over the heavy metal.

The man shook his head and lay back down.

"As you can see, my front door's lock was broken."

"Are there any other doors?"

"Nope. Just replace that one. I have my client," he motioned over his shoulder. "I need to get back to him."

"I'm set," Blondie said as he opened his toolbox and started work.

*Slap.*

Blondie looked over to the sling and saw a red handprint across the man's bare ass. Pat slipped on a black rubber glove that went all the way up to his elbow. He smiled at Blondie. He winked as he slid on the other glove. He bent over, showing his hairy ass in all its glory. His tight, sinewy muscles rippled. A deep dimple was visible on each cheek. A thick line of hair trailed down his crease.

Blondie stroked his screwdriver as he watched Pat dip his hand into a can and remove a fistful of thick, white cream. BUTT BUTTER was written on the side of the container.

Pat spread it up one glove and took the excess to the man's tight ass. He smeared it on the pink hole and pressed a finger to it. The naked man's body tensed.

Blondie had the door's hole open, and he slipped his fingers in to clean it out. All of the wood and metal scraps were removed as he explored the opening.

Pat slipped one finger in and circled the opening. He smeared the cream round and round. He slipped another finger in and circled again.

Blondie pushed the dead bolt into the door and positioned it in the center of the hole. He could feel his body starting to respond.

Pat shaped his fingers into a cone and pressed the tips to the tight opening.

Blondie picked up the doorknob shaft and admired the length. He carefully lined it up with the dead bolt and gently slipped it into place.

Pat's hand disappeared into the man and held firm.

Blondie placed the flip side of the doorknob on the outside. He maneuvered them together and pressed hard. A metallic snap echoed in the room, making all three men jump. His fingers fumbled with the screws to secure the knob.

Pat inserted his hand deeper and pulled out. A wet suction popped, and he plunged his hand in again, easier and deeper this time. He repeated the process and drove in deeper and longer.

The naked man moaned with pleasure. His legs jerked in the stirrups and his hands clung to the downward supports. "Deeper, harder," he begged in a low growl.

Blondie screwed as Pat plunged. Sweat broke out across his brow and burned his eyes as he wiped it away with the back of his hand. He tried the doorknob and spun it several times. He inserted the key and removed it. Lock open, lock closed. Unlocked, locked.

Pat's arm slid in, up to his midforearm. His puppet convulsed in the sling as they started to rock back and forth.

Blondie finished and cleaned up his mess. He removed an invoice from his clipboard and found a new set of keys. He left his toolbox at the door and stepped over to them.

Pat motioned to the small table in the corner. "Set them over there."

"Anything else?" Blondie asked.

A smile played over Pat's lips. "Could you apply the nipple clamps?" He tipped his head to the metal tray of dildos. Two long metal clamps shone in the light.

Sweat and sex, leather and lube filled the air around the naked man. Blondie touched one of the cool metal tools that looked like a surgical instrument. He played with the opening mechanism and stroked the hard, cold metal over one nipple.

The naked man jerked at the unexpected touch and looked at the tool. "Yes."

Blondie circled his nipple and it rose into a sharp point. He guided the tip to the swollen end and pinched it. He teased it and watched as it grew bigger. He squeezed down on the clamp and it clicked, locked on its prey. The angry pink nipple deepened to red and then purple. He picked up the other clamp and ran this one over the man's hard cock. He pulled the foreskin back and spread the precum over the end and down the shaft.

"Good," Pat cooed as he pulled out and dove back in.

A splat of butt butter fell out of his client's opening and landed on the floor.

Blondie trailed the clamp up the naked torso and over to the other nipple. He bent over and licked the bump. As he rolled it between his teeth, blood filled the tip, and it rose up in his mouth. He sucked hard on him, tasting man and muscle. Blondie stood up and teased the tip with the metal. He circled the colored area and worked to the point. He opened the mouth of the clamp and pinched. His saliva made the metal slip off, and he had to grab a larger bite to make it stay. He squeezed the metal and it clicked into place.

Pat drove his arm in farther, and the depression of his elbow almost cupped the man's balls.

"You're good," Pat said. "I could always use another hand." He pointed at the eight-inch cock flopping back and forth.

Blondie winked and picked up a lube bottle. He poured some over the tip as if he was covering a sundae. He set the bottle down and grabbed the cock. He squeezed hard, making the pink turn red. He milked it a few times as more precum poured out. With each stroke down, the foreskin covered the penis's tip, and then when pulled back, it revealed the fat end.

Pat matched his strokes as he pulled on his red jock and

released his cock from the pouch. His balls flopped out and dangled low. They swung in rhythm with the penetration. He put his whole body into motion.

Blondie jacked the thick cock and watched as its balls pulled up alongside of the shaft. He pulled the foreskin down and a thick stream of cum exploded out of the end. It shot across the man's chest, over his nipple clamps and hit his chin.

The man threw his head back and let out a scream that echoed down to the core of Blondie's balls. He continued to stroke his shaft, sending another wave out and over. More semen boiled out and ran down the shaft. He milked the sensitive organ and watched as the man's body tensed and released. He looked like he had passed out, but his moan continued as Pat drove deeper in.

"Thanks," Pat said.

Blondie shook the excess cum off his hand back onto the man and looked around for a towel.

Pat motioned behind him to the one dangling from his chaps.

Blondie used it and rubbed up against his bare ass. "Love the hairy ass, man."

"Come back when you're done with my brothers. We'll still be here." He puckered his mouth, and Blondie kissed him long, hard and deep.

Blondie knocked on the next door and waited. Barry Manilow played on the stereo. A stocky man answered the door. "Hello," Matt Kodiak said. He wore tight shorts and a half T-shirt. He was huskier and hairier then his brother bear.

"I'm Blondie, I'm here to install the new locks."

"Come in, come in. We're filming a movie as I bake bread and do some cleaning. These break-ins have upset my household." He tucked a rag into his back pocket and wiped his hands on the red plaid apron he wore. The apron was small, barely able to cover the bulge in his shorts.

Blondie looked around the living room. Lace curtains covered the windows, shadow boxes filled with tea cups and saucers covered the walls, and doilies covered each table and the back of each seat in the room.

Blondie felt as if he had stepped into his grandmother's house. Potpourri sat in glass bowls and fruity, flowery scents hung in the air. He inhaled deeply. No bread yet.

"The back door was where he entered last night, but I would like a dead bolt on the front door too." Matt pointed to the door Blondie had just entered.

"We're filming in here," Matt said, as they walked into the kitchen. A grown man sat in an adult-size baby chair. All he wore was a diaper. His long hairy legs were muscular; his hairy chest was tan and sculpted. Mushy food was smeared over his face and caked on his chest. A video camera recorded what was happening in the kitchen.

Matt turned to him. "Baby, we'll be right back."

Blondie nodded at the man and followed Matt. The back door was in the other corner of the kitchen. The door was unmarred, but the doorknob hung out of the hole. "Any damage to the door?"

"Surprisingly, no."

The man-baby slapped his high-chair tray, spilling his milk.

Matt scolded, "Don't be a bad baby, eat your food."

The man-baby picked up his tippy cup and poured the orange juice into his diaper.

"Anything I can get you before you start?" Matt asked.

"No, I'm good. I'll run out to my truck and get a second lock and start in the living room." Blondie left before Matt could say anything else.

Blondie finished the front door in fifteen minutes and entered the kitchen, afraid of what he'd see. Avoiding the camera, he made his way to the back door.

More food covered the "baby," and Matt picked up a large pacifier and slipped it into his mouth. "Be a good baby."

The baby took the pacifier out and threw it on the floor. "Wet." He pointed to his soaked diaper.

"Let's go to the bedroom, and we can change that."

"No."

"You want it changed here?"

Matt glanced over at Blondie. Blondie shrugged his shoulders and opened the back door. He quickly started to remove the broken knob.

Matt unhooked a large diaper pin, and a thick bush of hair came into view. He opened the other side, and an eight-inch hard-on stood proudly under the tray.

Blondie gasped at the sight.

Matt smiled, opened a drawer, and took out a package of baby wipes. He wiped the baby's chest and worked lower.

Blondie half watched, half worked on the doorknob. Sweat broke out over his body, as cool beads ran down his back and into his underwear. He could feel his cock swell and grow.

Matt turned to throw the wipe away as the baby stood up in the chair. As Matt turned around, the baby pointed to his butt. His butt was white and smooth, showing Speedo tan lines.

"Do you have a poopy butt?" Matt took another wipe and washed up his crease and then spread out to cover his cheeks.

The baby cried, and Matt picked up his pacifier. The man-baby turned his head away and stuck his butt toward him. Matt dipped the pacifier into the butter on the table and pressed it between the man-baby's butt cheeks. It slipped in easily, and Matt pulled it out and pushed it in, over and over again.

Blondie felt his cock swell in his jeans. He reached down and adjusted himself.

"More," the baby said.

Matt picked up the other man and set him on the table. He let the baby's legs hang off the edge and stood between them. He quickly unzipped his shorts, which fell to the floor. He stepped out of them and reached into the pocket on the apron. He removed a condom and slipped it on. A bottle of lube sat in the center of the table. He applied a coating over his cock and pulled out the pacifier.

Baby brought his legs up, and Matt poured lube between his cheeks.

"Did you want to join us?" Matt asked. "Baby could use a new pacifier to suck on."

"I'm almost done here," Blondie said, as he screwed the last one into place. He stood and tried the doorknob.

Matt slipped his dick into the man-baby and held his hairy legs around his neck. He humped his backside as his hand curled around man-baby's shaft. He stroked up and down his length.

Man-baby moaned and bucked his hips.

Blondie gathered his tools and placed them in his toolbox. He tossed the broken lock into the garbage can and pulled out his receipt book.

Matt quickened his pace.

Blondie ripped off the bill and set it on the table.

Man-baby moaned, "Faster, faster."

"You're more than welcome to stay...."

"Ah, ah, ah," man-baby said and shot his load across his hairy chest.

Matt pumped into him a few more times and came hard. His body flopped over onto man-baby's body.

"It's getting late, besides I need to get to your brother's

house." Blondie tossed the new set of keys on the table. "Let me know if anything is not *just* right. Phone number's on the invoice." And he left to go next door, pulling his underwear away from his sticky body.

Blondie wondered what the third brother would be like as he knocked on the door.

No loud music blared from inside. One light burned in the front window, but no movement could be detected.

He knocked again, louder this time.

Heavy footfalls approached the door, and Bart Kodiak opened the door in a white robe. His hairy legs and chest contrasted nicely with the fluffy white. Not quite as big as his older brothers, Bart appeared to be more an otter than a bear, but definitely a cub in training.

"You must be Blondie, come in," Bart extended his hand and firmly shook the locksmith's.

Blondie stepped inside and inhaled deeply: Lemon Pledge and wood smoke. In the living room, a fire burned in the huge fireplace adding a welcoming touch to the house. Thick carpet covered the floor, as overstuffed chairs looked into the hearth. Wooden bookshelves lined the walls and were filled with leather-bound volumes and colorful best sellers.

"You look surprised," Bart said.

"I just finished your brothers' locks."

Bart smiled and nodded. "Their jobs take them into a different world than the one I live in." He shifted his weight from one leg to the other. His robe opened slightly to reveal more calf and thigh.

Blondie forced his eyes to look away.

"You can look. I'm an artist. I'm used to people looking at me and my work."

Blondie felt his face burn and knew he was blushing like a schoolgirl.

"Sorry to embarrass you. The front and back doors need new locks. When you finish the front door, go through the kitchen and turn right. I'll be in the room to the left."

"Okay," Blondie said, and started work. He finished changing the front doorknob in record time, especially without any distractions. He looked down at the white carpet and took off his work boots. He set them on the tiled entryway and padded into the kitchen. No oversize baby–high chairs sat in any corner. Maybe this brother was normal.

He continued down the hall and paused at the door on the left. Canvases that stretched from floor to ceiling lined the walls, and a plastic tarp covered the floor. Cans and small jars of paint sat in neat rows on a rolling cart.

Bart reclined on the floor and stared at one canvas. He startled when he looked to the door.

"Sorry to scare you," Blondie said.

"I was off in my little world, daydreaming in color. I'm trying to see what wants to be painted tonight, but nothing is calling to me."

"Waiting for inspiration to strike?"

Bart let out a deep breath. "It's hard to be creative after your home has been violated." He motioned to the back door, which was hidden by his canvas. "Oops, let me move that." He pushed up to his feet and picked up the canvas. He set it in front of a canvas on another wall.

Blondie walked over to the door and started removing the smashed knob.

Bart stared at him as he worked. He admired his nimble fingers and form; he sighted him with his hands, framing him at different angles.

Blondie paused and looked at Bart.

Bart froze in midframe.

"Caught ya," Blondie said.

"Just curious," Bart said. "You have such fluidity with your body, I was trying to figure out how I could capture that movement in paint."

Blondie continued to work, observing Bart from the corner of his eye. As he moved around the room, Blondie realized Bart was naked underneath the robe.

"Be back in a second," Bart said, and left the room. He returned with two cold beers, one of which he handed to Blondie as he took a long drag on his.

Blondie looked up at him. "I don't drink on the job."

"Looks to me like you are almost done." He waved the bottle back and forth. "Come on, you know you want it. You're thirsty, I can tell."

Blondie tightened the last screw. He set his tools in the chest and tossed the broken doorknob into the box. As he reached over and took the bottle, his hand brushed against Bart's hand for a second, and he felt electricity soar through his body.

Bart felt it too.

Blondie clinked their beer bottles together and took a long swallow. He didn't realize how thirsty he had been.

"I got it!" Bart smiled and turned to look Blondie in the eyes. "But I'll need your help." Bart's deep brown eyes held Blondie's hazel ones. He watched as they swirled from a greenish tint to amber. "Your eyes change color with your mood," Bart uttered his words in a sensuous purr.

"I still have to get to Thomas's…"

"He called me before you arrived and canceled. His son needed a project for shop class, so they worked on their door together."

Blondie looked at him, not sure whether he should believe him or not.

"Trust me, would I lie to you? Besides, it's almost midnight."

Blondie glanced at his watch and saw he was right.

"I really need some help, please stay."

Bart handed him a jar of paint and let his robe fall to the floor. He turned his back to Blondie. "Pour the paint over my back."

Blondie poured the paint over his shoulder, behind his neck and over to the other shoulder. He watched as the cold paint cascaded over the golden brown skin and washed over the artist's beautiful bubble-butt.

He shuffled over to the canvas and pressed his butt against it. He smeared his body across the fabric.

Blondie's eyes drank in Bart's body: deep tan, sculpted muscles, perfect hair pattern and a big endowment.

Bart walked over to the cart and picked up a burnt red bottle. "Your turn." He shook it.

"What?"

"Take off your clothes."

"I...I...can't."

Bart moved closer, paint still dripping from his body. "If you don't, you'll get dirty." He smiled, "Actually, you'll get dirty if you take them off too. At least your clothes won't be ruined."

Blondie tried to escape, but Bart blocked his exit. "Strip."

Blondie unbuttoned his shirt. "I really should go," he protested.

Bart pulled his arm back as if to throw the paint.

Blondie took off his shirt and threw it into the hall. He unhooked his belt and pants, which he shed quickly. His briefs flew out of the room, and he stood naked, waiting.

Bart stepped forward and poured.

The cold red paint flowed over Blondie's chest, and Bart guided his body to the canvas. He pushed and painted the canvas with Blondie, both hands on his ass to control the outcome.

Blondie's cock grew hard along the away, and an upward arc swelled and grew.

"Beautiful. Pour the forest green over my chest," Bart commanded.

Blondie dumped the container on Bart's chest and watched it slowly run down his torso. A wave washed over his pubic hair and coated the jungle.

A splash flew onto Blondie's chest, and he ducked back.

"It's all good," Bart said smiling. He emptied the Swedish blue over Blondie. "I want us to roll across the canvas on the floor." Bart lay on the edge of one, rolled over until he fell off the other end. He motioned for Blondie to do the same.

As he stood up, Bart hugged him.

"You're mixing colors," Blondie warned.

"I'm making them the perfect blend."

"Is that what you call it?" Blondie laughed.

"Come on, I have a few more." He opened another jar and poured it across Blondie's butt. "Sit on that one and scoot your butt across."

"You're serious."

"I am. I know what I'm doing."

"Aren't these small jars of paint expensive?"

"I prefill them with the colors I want to work with and measure how much I need so I don't waste hardly any." He picked up an open container that had sat for a while. "The excess I can splatter or pour or whatever and add a little splash here and there." He showed him by adding the burnt red to a few places on a few of the pictures. He handed one jar to Blondie. "Have at it."

"I don't know what I'm doing."

"Neither do I, just have fun and throw. See what happens. Like this." Bart threw the last of a jar on Blondie and then pressed him against the wall. He smeared his butt along the canvas as he resisted, then Bart turned him to face it and ran Blondie's erection along the length of the screen. A bold splash of red proudly stood out.

Bart added more streaks and sprays of color over the paintings. Foot and handprints, butt and cock-prints, arm and leg-prints with hairy appendages added texture and depth to the art. He pushed Blondie down on top of the canvas and joined him. He rubbed his body against Blondie's. His hand reached down and stroked his thick penis.

Blondie threw his back in pleasure. The paint, the canvas, and Bart had aroused him. "I'm going to…" was all he said.

"I hope you do, shoot it all over."

Blondie's orgasm hit hard. His whole body jerked and a thick load of cum sprayed across the paint.

"Perfect," Bart said, as he continued to jack his cock.

Blondie's arms and legs dropped to his side as he lay spent in the paint.

"The paint's gone," Bart said, turning to Blondie. "Now comes the fun part."

Blondie looked confused.

"The cleanup." Bart took his hand and led him to the mudroom. A huge shower stall stood wide open. "Get in."

Blondie stepped in, and Bart turned on the water. Sprays of hot water shot out of the walls and from the ceiling. Steam rose and filled the space. Streaks of color ran over their skin and swirled down the drain.

Bart reached into the corner shelf and removed a bottle of body wash and a loofah sponge. He soaped it up and started to scrub Blondie's back, his broad shoulders, his rippled lats. As bare flesh emerged, colored foam flowed downward. "Bend over," he commanded.

The sponge washed over one tight cheek and rode the crease between. Blondie moaned.

"This won't fit, so I'll have to use something else," Bart said into his ear. He soaped up his hard-on and guided it between Blondie's cheeks. Its length drilled in deep and scrubbed up and down.

His hands reached around and washed Blondie's chest. His fingers worked the paint and the soap into a colorful foam, which the sprays washed down. He poured a palm full of shampoo and ran his fingers through the short blond hair.

Then Blondie washed Bart, scrubbing every inch of his body, even checking behind each ear. As his clean naked body glowed, Blondie drew him down to the stall's floor. He picked him up and placed his cock between his cheeks. He carefully lowered Bart down on his dick; slowly he entered.

Bart relaxed and breathed deeply, as he rode the locksmith's pelvis. Blondie grabbed Bart's cock and soaped its length. As he entered Bart, he stroked his dick. Long, slow, hard and firm, he worked the erect flesh in his hand.

As his sensation increased, so did his speed. Bart sat down harder on Blondie, slamming his ass down, impaling himself.

Blondie bucked his hips and forced himself deeper into Bart.

Tingles turned to waves, which soon exploded between the two men, Blondie filling Bart's ass, as Bart emptied his balls across Blondie's chest. The water continued to wash over them, as the steam swirled around.

As their breathing returned to normal, Bart stood up and pulled two fluffy towels off the rack. He wrapped one around his waist and walked over to Blondie. He beckoned him to leave the shower and started to dry him.

Blondie unwrapped Bart's waist and dried him, enjoying the April-fresh scents that dried their bodies.

"Follow me," Bart said, dropping his towel to the floor. He led Blondie to his bed, and both men snuggled under the down comforter. He kissed him as they settled into each other's arms.

"I hope everything is just right," Blondie said, as his body molded to Bart and together, they melted into the mattress that formed to them, just right.

So, the house was locked up, nice and tight.

And Blondie stayed over, all night.

# SERVICE CALL

Marvin Richmond

The good thing about those phone/Internet/cable combination packages is that they are relatively inexpensive and you only have one bill to pay for all three services. The bad thing, however, is that sometimes when one thing goes down, everything goes down, instantly shoving you right back into the Dark Ages.

That's what happened to me. I'd been dead in the water all weekend. Looking forward to a three-day weekend and tired from working overtime, I came home Friday night to find a snowstorm on every TV channel, no dial tone on the landline, and, worst of all, no wireless connection. I was about ready to kill myself—how could I possibly survive without the Internet? I contacted the phone company using my cell and really got pissed off when they told me the earliest they could send someone out was Monday. How did they expect a human being to survive without media access to the outside world for almost three whole days?

I did what I could to deal with it. I contacted some friends and bar-hopped Friday night. Using my laptop, I sucked up caffeine and wireless from the neighborhood coffee shop on Saturday, sending emails and chatting with friends. I went to my old video store for the first time in years, amazed that I remembered my customer number, and checked out some DVDs. Sitting outside my closed, but still transmitting wireless local library on Sunday morning, I visited my favorite blogs and updated Facebook. I even spent some time just walking around the neighborhood over the weekend, enjoying the mild, early fall weather. Time would have gone faster if I'd had a partner or even a fuck buddy to hook up with, of course, but still, once I got over the withdrawal symptoms, and my hand and fingers stopped shaking from their desire to click a mouse or a button on the remote control, I almost got used to being unplugged. Almost.

I was surprised and confused when the doorbell rang early Monday morning. I was semi-awake anyway—and semierect, my thumb hovering over the PLAY button on the DVD remote. Waking up lazy, alone and horny, with no job to report to that day, I was all set to replay the one very good scene in an otherwise dull XXX movie that I'd picked up at the video store to rid myself of my usual morning hard-on. "Damn," I said aloud, dropping both the remote and my own fat shaft. "Who the hell is this?" I quickly threw on some sweatpants and a shirt and hurried downstairs.

"You put in a service call?" a young man asked when I opened the door. A white van sat at the curb in front of the building. I blinked, stuttered and nodded then mumbled yes. I had forgotten about my electronic problems and frankly had not expected someone to show up so early. I'd also expected one of those older, out-of-shape guys they usually send, not this lanky, attractive homeboy. About six three and chestnut brown, he couldn't have been much beyond his midtwenties. The wisp of moustache and goatee he'd grown, framing a small, perfectly shaped mouth, did manage to make him look a touch less like a teenager. Only the frigid morning air icing through my thin sweats stopped the reappearance of my erection as I stepped aside, letting the repairman in.

"You know, you didn't sign up for the extended service contract with us," he said, glancing down at his paperwork. "If the problem's inside, you'll have to pay."

"Yeah, yeah, that's okay," I said nodding. "I need my Internet, man. I'm at the top of the stairs."

"I heard that," he nodded and clumped up the stairs to my apartment. I live in what was once some rich guy's summer house back when this part of the city was still the country, which has been converted into three apartments. My neighbors were either asleep or out of town. The only noise in the building seemed to be the sound of the keys, tools and diagnostic equipment jangling from the young man's broad tan work belt and slapping against his hips.

*Damned baggy jeans,* I thought, following behind him, my eyes falling from the broad belt down to his steel-toed work boots and back up again. Even though he wore his pants a size too large, like most young inner-city guys, I could still detect the outline of a full and satisfying ass. I shook my head and ran a hand over my face as we entered my small apartment. *I'm still asleep,* I thought, attempting to rid my mind of cobwebs. *I need to snap out of it, wake myself up.* It was too early in the morning for me to be lusting after some probably straight young boy.

Fortunately, the cable and Internet connections were in the front room of my apartment, so he didn't have to go back into my messy bedroom. We pulled the couch out from the wall, and he dropped down behind it to take a look.

As he sat on his haunches, the back of his oversized pants slipped down to reveal more of his gray and white boxers, their band ringed with the repeated name of a famous closeted clothing designer. I recognized them—I had a pair just like them—and smiled, watching his smooth-shaven head move from side to side as he worked, and I felt a stirring in my sweats. I quickly turned and tried to adjust myself. I didn't need the embarrassment of showing this guy that I'd thrown a rod as I watched his long fingers checking connections.

He didn't need me hanging around, and I thought I should at least try to straighten up the place. I hit the ON button on the radio to give us both something to listen to while we worked. A local college radio morning show, a soothing mix of cool jazz and soft pop, began flowing from the speakers. I went into the kitchen and washed the dishes that I'd just piled in the sink the night before and began to put things away. Just as I'd finished, the repairman walked in, his tall frame filling the doorway. "Looks like the problem's not in your line, bro. I've got to go outside."

"Okay." I looked at him for a moment, imagining tilting my head up to kiss his sweet young lips as he stood there, to thank him for his efforts, and just as quickly I put that thought away. "You can just close that outside door downstairs and leave it unlocked to get in and out, if you want," I managed to say without stumbling over my words. I looked away from the repairman's suddenly intense stare.

"Cool," the young man nodded, and clumped and jangled back down the stairs.

Once he was gone, at first I thought I'd begin tackling the bedroom. It really was ridiculous how I'd just left clothes lying where I'd taken them off for the past few days. But I'd been whipped from the overtime I'd worked and just wasn't in the mood to do much more than come home and sleep. This weekend was the first in a long time that I had completely to myself.

A remote control clattered to the floor when I lifted the spread to make the bed. The sound reminded me that I'd left TV and the DVD stopped in my rush to answer the door. My dick stirred slightly. This was the real reason why the young repairman had gotten me so worked up, I thought. I had been perhaps too much by myself in recent months. I had been all set to get off when he rang the bell. I listened carefully, checking to see if he had maybe returned, but heard nothing. *Just one quick peek,* I thought, pressing the PLAY button.

The screen flickered and then jumped to reveal a dark chocolate African American dick plowing into a firm, light-brown Latino ass. Both were wearing leather and chain harnesses and tall engineer's boots, with the bottom boy's butt framed by chaps, and the screen was practically filled with the scent of lust and danger. The black man grunted as he forced his way into the other's tight opening. "Fuck me, papi," the Latino sighed, his wincing face relaxing into a look of pleasure as he got used to being intensely reamed out. My eyes were riveted to the screen as I watched the two hot actors going at it. I'd watched this one scene at least three times already by then but still enjoyed every minute of it. I reached into my sweats and began stroking myself.

I don't know if it was my own natural versatility or just indecisiveness that caused me to mentally shift back and forth as I watched, pulling on myself, identifying with both actors. At times I wished I were the taller, thicker brotha, holding tight to a pair of perfect light-brown hips while I sawed my way into a sweet *culo.* At other times, I imagined myself on my hands and knees, whimpering as a thick black cock pounded into me. If I could somehow insert myself between the two of them, become the filling in a black-black-brown male sandwich, I'd be completely satisfied. The thought of fucking one guy while getting fucked by his partner got me very excited, and I reached my right hand up under my sweatshirt to pinch my nipples, while pumping my now rigid dick faster with my left.

A rattling sound coming through the windows from the backyard snapped me awake. The repair guy! I'd forgotten that he might be coming back into the apartment at any minute. I turned off the DVD, leaving it in for after my guest had gone and continued making up the bed.

I had just about gotten the bedroom looking fit for human habitation when I heard the repairman coming back up the stairs. I went out to meet him.

"Okay, the problem was in the lines outside, so there was no charge," he said. "You just need to sign this to prove that I was here, and I'll be on my way."

"Great," I said, glad not to have to spend more money I didn't have anyway. "Thanks."

Handing me a clipboard, he coughed. "You know, I have that problem first thing in the morning too, man...."

I blinked. "What...what problem?"

He smiled slyly and pulled up his slipping jeans. "You know what I mean. I had to go outside, right, fix your connection? Had to get the ladder, go up on the pole outside the house to get to it. I was right outside your window." He nodded behind me. "I saw what you was doing."

A cold flush swept through my body. My gaze dropped to the floor and I began stuttering.

"Hey, hey, hey...it's cool, yo!" The repairman's smile broadened into grin. "Like I said, I do it, too. We all get that morning hard-on, ya know what I mean? It's no big deal."

"Yeah, well...but still. I just forgot that you were out there." I smiled sheepishly, shrugged and chuckled, wiping a line of sweat from my forehead, and began to walk him out of the apartment.

"Were you watching a video or something?" he asked as we headed down the stairs. His voice was friendly enough, but the sound of work boots clumping down the steps right behind me was a little unnerving.

"Ye...yeah" I said, my voice shaking.

"Thought so. I could see you pulling on it and standing in front of the TV and all, but I couldn't see the screen. Good scene, huh?"

I mumbled sounds of assent, wondering where this conversation was heading. The memory of the video stirred my still unrelieved member.

"I used to do that, but my DVD player stopped working. Gotta use my own imagination for now, you know. I wake up every morning and my jimmy's hard as shit!" He laughed. His voice seemed to suddenly deepen when he said, "Sure wish I had some nice visuals to look at. Or some friend to help me out—know what I mean?"

I had reached the bottom of the stairs. I turned to look back at this guy. He was already taller than I was, but standing two steps above me he seemed to loom over me like a thin black tower. Perhaps turning around just then was not the best thing to do, as I was now at eye level with his denim-covered crotch. One of his hands casually pulled at the tower hidden there as well, which was straining the fabric, begging to be released. My own maleness tented my sweats in imitation of his, yearning to finish what I had started earlier before being interrupted.

I couldn't help but lick my lips. "Well, hmm..." I looked up into the young man's brown eyes and smiled. "Maybe you could find someone to help you out. I mean...it would be terrible if you came out all this way and didn't get some kind of payment for your work. I didn't even offer you a cup of coffee." I placed my hand over his bulging member. "Or something…"

I could feel his hardness jumping eagerly beneath my hand. "Don't like coffee too much," he said quietly. "Tell you what I do like…" He guided my hand toward his zipper. Together we slowly lowered it.

I was startled by the thickness of the slab of meat he hauled out of his pants. Because the rest of his body was tall and thin, I expected his dick to be the same. Instead, it was certainly long enough, nine or ten inches, but it was thick as the handle of one of the tools hanging from his belt. It was darker than the rest of his body, too, with a plump round head, growing from a full mat of pubic hair.

"Damn," I whispered, hypnotized by the slowly waving Cyclops in front of me. I leaned in and began to slowly caress it, licking cautiously at the eye with my tongue. I knew I wanted to enjoy this young man's offering slowly and started with quick kisses along its length. Increasing my contact with his dick, I carefully licked across his piss slit and around it, then dove under him to lick the entire length of his shaft from underneath. The repairman shuddered each time my wet tongue touched his smooth, hot skin and reached to cup my head in both his hands, face-fucking me, forcing me to take all of him in.

His hands were warm and large, the hard tips of his calloused fingers scratching the skin beneath my ears. They covered the entire side of my face, and I moaned as he pumped into me, giving only token resistance. I closed my eyes and gladly opened my mouth wide, trying to swallow the repairman in one greedy gulp, getting only about two thirds of his thickness inside me on the first try as he rolled his hips. It was very satisfying to finally feel his head hit the back of my throat, curly pubic hairs scratching my nose.

"Damn, homeboy—you sure like to suck dick, don't you?" the young guy whispered. I growled in agreement, knowing he would be able to feel the vibrations in his shaft. "Fuck, that shit feels good! Lemme get more comfortable here." He lowered his jeans and boxers to his ankles and sat down on the carpeted steps, spreading his legs. His eyes bored a hole right through me while I pulled down my sweatpants and stepped out of them. He wrapped both hands around the base of his dick, wiggling it at me.

I hardly needed the encouragement. The sight of him spread out there on the steps was irresistible. I rubbed his smooth, nearly hairless legs, then dove between them. Instead of going for his dick, I went straight to his balls. Hanging low in their wrinkled basket, they looked so lonely, in desperate need of some attention. Judging from the way the repairman jumped and sighed as I bathed them with my mouth, I was right. His young musk also intrigued me, and I turned my head as much as I could to inhale the pungent aroma as I held him in my mouth. I opened my mouth wide, allowing saliva to ooze down the dark path between his balls and hidden asshole. Letting his eggs drop, working his dark tower with my left hand, I followed my spit under him with my mouth. The repairman scooted down a bit, giving me easier access to his ass. I inhaled deeply as I went, growing light-headed with his strong scent that overpowered the residue of the soap he'd used during his morning shower. I kissed his semicircular asscheeks and licked into the crack between them. He gasped sharply but didn't object. In fact, he spread his legs even more, stretching the fabric of his jeans and underwear around his ankles.

Using both hands, I spread his cheeks and began to seriously lick the young boy's winking star. He wriggled, sucked air and said, "Shit...damn!! DAMN!" over and over as I cleaned out his brown hole. His rock-solid penis wavered over me like a dancing cobra as I ate his ass for breakfast.

I began to wonder how serious he had been about not seeing what I had been watching in the bedroom. How else could he know I might be interested in doing something with another man? I quickly put those thoughts out of my mind and closed my eyes and began to dream. I imagined stripping him completely of his pants, leaving only his work boots and utility belt, then lifting his legs and fucking his tight young ass. I could almost feel our sloppy kisses on my mouth, my tongue searching for his tonsils as his long, brown legs wrapped around me. The heavy boots bounced against my hunching ass as I drove my jimmy into him. His head rolled slowly from side to side, his face even more beautiful with his eyes closed and wincing slightly as I banged his prostrate, his mouth open in a satisfied moan of ecstasy.

But then I thought, *No*. The guy was probably straight or wanted me to think so. I'd played this down low game before. A little mouth action he could handle but not me sticking my dick in his ass—not on our first encounter, anyway. But what about the other way around? The feel of him filling my mouth already had my asshole twitching with envy. I pulled his dick from my throat and began to stroke it, rubbing it against my face before diving down to lick his balls again, swirling my tongue around his sac, sucking it in. I jacked him with my hand, imagining the telephone repairman's thick pole pushing deep inside me, sweetly answering my call. I moaned at the thought.

"You like that?" I asked. He mumbled something unintelligible, lost in the cleaning my tongue was giving his low-hangers. "You want to try something else?" Again I smeared his wet dick across my face. I tightened my lips and slowly parted them with his dick, trying to imitate a tight hole with my mouth. "Maybe you'd like a little ass before you go," I said, coming up for air.

He coughed. "Uhh…I'm sorry, man, but I don't go that way." The young man leaned up on his elbows. "Don't get me wrong—I'm not knocking you if you like that shit. And," he leaned over and looked behind me, "you do got a nice butt and all…but I can't do that. Sorry. This is cool, tho.… Is it okay with you? I'm pretty close to shooting anyway."

Cool? It was more than cool with me. In fact, I was very hot and close to cumming myself. My dick was now leaking a steady stream of precum. Only slightly disappointed, I returned to breakfast between his legs.

The young man wasn't kidding about being close. No sooner had I gotten back to sucking him in earnest than his legs began to quiver. He humped his butt up off the steps insistently, pumping his thickness deeper into my mouth. He placed one hand around its base, the other on the top of my head forcing me down. I suppose I could have objected, but I didn't. In fact, I wouldn't have minded getting a mouthful of this guy's sweet young cream. I lifted my sweatshirt and began pinching at my hard nipples with one hand, pulling on my own crying dick with the other. I drove my head farther onto his cock, impaling myself, willing out his tender seed.

"Damn, I'm gonna cum, yo… I'm'a cum!" he cried. He pushed my greedy mouth away and jacked himself in a frenzy. His tower spit, one glob popping from its opening, then gushed like an erupting volcano, spilling thick white lava down his dark shaft and over his still-pumping fingers, leaving thick droplets on the carpeted step.

I wanted badly to lean down and lap up his sweet honey with my tongue but restrained myself. Both my hands were now on my dick, urging it to follow him into paradise. I let one hand slide under my aching dick and balls to finger my asshole. If I couldn't have this young man inside me or be inside him, at least I could imagine it.

The repairman stared, still milking his dick, then surprised me. He leaned up and lifted my sweatshirt. He glanced up at me and began to pinch my nipples. My head fell back and I shuddered as he began to lick my left nipple. Then he moved over and began to kiss and nibble the right one as well. The feel of his hot tongue lapping at my chest was electric.

I looked down and couldn't help myself: I had to kiss the young man's forehead to thank him for giving me such pleasure. He shook his head in protest the minute my lips touched his lightly sweat-glazed skin. I sighed. *Yeah, right,* I thought: *"Straight" means "no kissing."* I leaned back but put one hand behind his neck to pull him closer. For some reason, he didn't object to that and began to chew in earnest on my chest, driving me to the edge of an explosion.

Then his hands, which had been holding my torso to him as he fed, dropped to my bare ass. He kneaded my brown butt roughly, and I began to wonder whether he'd maybe changed his mind about having a piece of my ass. But he just continued to squeeze and flex, fingers slowly sliding toward my crack. I grunted when they first brushed against the damp crevice and I rolled my hips. His fingers played again in my moist opening then dove in, searching for my hole. Hot and ready from hours of excitement that had started with my DVD watching, my pucker sucked greedily as his finger neared it. With a sudden, welcome jab, the young repairman shoved one of his long fingers all the way inside me in one stroke.

That was all I needed to make me erupt. I cried in pain and pleasure. I came in spurts, my body jumping as my jizz leapt out like shots from my long-delayed gun. My asshole spasmed around the young man's wiggling finger, urging me to spill out all my treasure. He leaned back when I yelled to avoid being hit by my unleashed geyser but wasn't fast enough. One of my initial spurts caught him on the chin, and a few of my pearly drops glistened in his thin beard. My ejaculation filled my belly button, bathing my lower stomach in white. As my eruptions slowed to a dribble and then stopped, the young man slowly pulled his finger from my quivering asshole.

Swooning, I leaned into him. He moved his head away, afraid, I suppose, that I was going to try to kiss him again. I only wanted to lick my cum from his cheek and beard. Thinking that would probably freak him out, however, I stopped and just wiped it from his face with my hand, then leaned back against the wall and deeply sighed.

We both rested there half-naked for a while, completely spent. Then the repairman said, "I guess I better go." I nodded and started pulling on my sweats.

He wiped himself off with a checkered rag he'd pulled from the back pocket of his jeans, then offered it to me. I shook my head, wiping the jism on my stomach and pubes with the edge of my sweatshirt. "I gotta take a shower...need to do laundry anyway," I said. He nodded, stood and pulled up his pants. I stared at the now docile monster hanging between his legs. I was sorry to see it disappear beneath his jeans.

We walked silently to the door. I opened it. "You take care, man," I said as the young man left. "Yeah, you too, bro," he replied, not looking at me as he walked out the door.

I closed the door and sighed, then slowly struggled up the stairs to my apartment. The doorbell rang just as I'd reached the top.

"Now what?" I muttered, coming back down and opening the door. I jumped. The young repairman stood on the porch, looking a bit uneasy.

"What's the matter?" I asked. "Did you forget something?"

"Uh, well, I forgot to give you the receipt for the call...." He glanced around, again not looking me in the eye. "And I just...umm, well." A crumpled piece of paper was on top of the copy of the work order I'd signed. "You know, like—you ever have any more problems with your cable or whatever, you can give me a call. A'right, homeboy?" The look of gentle pleading in his eyes made me smile.

I gladly took both papers. "A'right," I nodded and closed the door. That would be one request for service I'd be more than happy to make.

# UNFINISHED BUSINESS

David Salcido

The school groundskeeper: he was the reason I was back. It took me a while to figure that one out, but there was nothing else in this crappy little town to draw me back here. It wasn't until I saw him, sharpening his scythe with a whetstone on the edge of the playground that I knew. Even as the schoolchildren cowered and moved away from him, just as they always had, I felt myself being drawn in. There was something deliciously malicious about old Willie. Something dangerous. Something exciting.

He still looked exactly the way I remembered him: disheveled, blazing red hair; bushy red beard; bulging, demented eyes and that trademark kilt. There was no way I could forget that kilt. Many a fevered dream had centered on that kilt. There was so much that remained a mystery about the man who wore it, even after all these years: his cloudy past, his barely suppressed anger, his legendary celibacy, his obsession with a long-forgotten murderer and a famous Scottish princess. He was, in a word, an enigma.

Once I realized that this man was the one I'd returned for, I followed him as he went about his business, skulking in the shadows like a stalker, awaiting my chance. That chance came later that night, as he sat next to a roaring fire outside his little wooden shack on the outskirts of the school grounds.

I took a deep breath and approached the fire. The Highlander ignored me. He was rolling a cigarette with stubby, calloused fingers that were a lot more graceful than they looked. He licked the edge of the paper and fixed me with heather green eyes, overshadowed by thick red brambles. In his strong Scottish brogue, he said something that sounded like, "Ken ay help yew, boyo?"

I stared straight into the inferno flickering in those eyes. "Do you remember me, Willie?"

He pondered, crimping the edges of the cigarette into tight prepuces. "Aye, I remember," he growled. "A real troublemaker, yew. I heard yew were sent away when yew were twelve, after being raped by the clown. Can't say as yew were missed." The humor in his voice was unmistakable. He was making fun of me, in his rough Highlander way. He stuck the entire cigarette in his mouth and pulled it out again, smoothing it with his generous lips.

"It wasn't the clown," I said evenly. "It was his sidekick."

Pulling a stick out of the fire, Willie expertly lit the cigarette, then jammed the stick back into the flames, causing sparks to rise up into the night and cast diabolical shadows on his craggy face. "A clown's a clown," he burred. "I also heard it wasn't rape. Some say he didn't deserve what he got."

I pondered the commentary. Willie was nothing if not truthful. And he didn't care how much that truth hurt. "He'd had it out for me for a long time," I said, trying to sound controlled and dangerous. "He deserved what he got, all right. Maybe not for doing that, but for other reasons."

Willie chuckled. "So, now yew're all grown up and back for more, ey, boyo? Bad news. No clowns here."

I ignored the dismissal and decided to get to the point. "I didn't come back for any clown. I came back to see you."

"Yew've seen me."

I hesitated, then plunged ahead. "I heard a few things, too, back then."

Willie didn't answer. He just inhaled deeply from his rolled cigarette and stared at me with that maniacal gleam in shadowed eyes.

"I heard that you're harboring a weapon of mass destruction under that kilt."

Willie smiled. "And yew thought yew'd come back here to find out?"

I didn't answer. It was the truth, forged by an incident in my youth, when I'd pranked Willie by lifting his kilt in a crowd of townsfolk. The reactions by those who'd witnessed the full brunt of the prank were indelibly imprinted onto my mind. The gasps would have been enough, but when one of the older women actually fainted, curiosity was born. That childhood curiosity had since grown to full-blown adult obsession.

Willie laughed, then leaned back and spread his hairy legs wide. The ubiquitous kilt rose and grew taut, perfectly framing a monstrous piece of meat, a wide fleshy canvas for the dancing flicker of the flames. A single drop of liquid hung poised on the edge of the puckered tip. I had never seen so much foreskin on one dick before. I was mesmerized.

Suddenly, Willie slammed his legs together again. The spell was broken. "That'll be enough of that, yew blouse-wearing lily-hugger. Yew've seen what yew came here to see. Now leave Willie in peace."

My mind raced. That couldn't be it. That couldn't possibly

be all there was. I hadn't come all this way to be turned away so easily. Then, as it had so often in the past, an idea popped into my fevered brain. Simple. Masterful. Sublime. "I have something for you, Willie."

The groundskeeper eyed me suspiciously, drawing deeply on his hand-rolled cigarette. "Yew've got nothing I need."

I swung my duffle bag off my back and set it on the ground, then dropped ceremoniously to one knee to rifle through it. Willie tensed, like a snake ready to strike, but watched me quietly. It was there somewhere. I dug deep seeking the key to unlocking Willie's resistance. My fingers settled on it and I clutched at it, pulling it from my duffle triumphantly. Willie stared at the prize I held aloft.

"Twine?" He sneered. "I've got spools of it in my shack."

"Not like this, you don't," I crowed. "This isn't just any twine. It's piano wire, strong and unbreakable as cable, yet thin enough to slice flesh. Perfect for the job *he* needed it for."

Willie cocked his head. "He...who?"

I had him! Now to deliver the coup de grace. "The Aberdeen Strangler."

I had to hand it to Willie. He didn't overreact and for a moment or two, and I thought I might have overplayed my hand. His eyes widened only slightly, then settled on the coil of wire in my hand. He stared at it, then dropped his maniacal gaze to meet my own.

"That's his own wire, is it?"

"The one and only."

"And how is it that yew have come into possession of such a prize, yew clown-humping blaggard?"

"I stumbled upon it by accident, while traveling through Europe." The story slowly unfolded in my head and I was carried away by it. "As luck would have it, I stopped into a Glasgow pub and fell into conversation with an older woman. A lovely thing she was, ruddy of complexion with a wild fall of red hair only just starting to fade with age. After a few pints, this lovely lass revealed to me that she was the only victim to survive the Strangler's grasp. The last victim. The one who turned the tables on him."

Willie's eyes grew increasingly wider. "The Duchess of York," he whispered almost reverentially. "Sarah Ferguson, herself?"

I had to stifle a laugh. "None other! I was invited back to her flat where we made passionate love for hours. Then, when I was dressing to leave, she told me that she wanted to give me something to remember her by. She pulled open a chest and pulled forth this cord; the very cord that had been used to strangle all of those innocent women. The cord that had almost spelled her own death! She entrusted it to me as a token of her affection."

"Yer lyin', boyo..." Willie growled.

"Am I?"

He stared at the coil of wire in my hand. "Are yew tellin' me yew sullied the grace and perfection of my Fergie?"

"Yes, but I did it for you, Willie!" I said dramatically. "I did it in honor of you!"

The groundskeeper was thrown off balance, unsure... "Fer me? How? Why?"

"I've been obsessed with you for years, Willie. I knew I couldn't have you, especially back then, but I knew I could have the next best thing. I could be you for one evening.

"And now that I'm back...I want to bestow on you this blessing which is rightfully yours."

Willie's bulging eyes narrowed and he swallowed hard. "Whut's yer price?"

I chuckled. "It's simple, Willie. Let me complete the circle. I've been you for an evening. Now I want to have you. All I ask is just one night and this holy relic will be yours. Forever."

Adrenaline pumped through my system as I teetered on the edge of the precipice. Would the old Scot take the bait I had so expertly laid out before him? Would he break his legendary vow of celibacy to own the one thing he'd never dreamed of possessing? Would he give it up for a piece of wire I'd stolen from my sister's grand piano last time I'd visited her?

The old man's lip curled and danger flickered in his fire lit eyes. "I know yew, boyo. Yew canna fool old Willie. It's a trick to make me lower my guard, so yew can make me the butt of one of ye'r cruel jokes. Yew and yer malicious friends..."

I lowered my hand and spoke so quietly the groundskeeper had to lean forward to hear me. "There's nobody here but us, Willie. You. Me. And the spirits of both the murderer you secretly admire and the woman you secretly love." I held the cord out toward him and watched his eyes fall hungrily upon it, as firelight played along its coiled lengths. "What'll it be? One night of passion for a lifetime of possession, or years of regret because you didn't take the offering that was yours for one brief moment?"

Turmoil played in the groundskeeper's wild eyes. He furrowed his brows angrily, then his face softened and his eyes grew watery. Still he remained silent. I nodded and slowly made to return the cord to its resting place deep within my duffle.

"Wait..." he said. I paused, not looking up. The cord hung poised just inches from the lip of the duffle, a fading memory retracting into bleak darkness.

"Promise me it's not some form of cruel joke," Willie whispered. "No cameras. No friends lurking in shadows. No newspaper reporters waiting to pounce..."

"You have my word, Willie. It's no joke."

He sighed and I looked up. Our eyes met and slowly his legs

parted again. This time, they stayed parted and the glory of his Highland broadsword lay revealed for my inspection. I stared at the offering triumphantly.

"Do with it what yew will, boyo," he whispered. "It is but flesh and not easily tempted, but to possess this holiest of relics, I will perform all manner of perversion." He stood and, in one swift movement, ripped his shirt open to reveal that magnificent rippled torso, blanketed with thick, curly red hair.

I nodded, dropping the cord into my bag and pulling the string taut. He watched it disappear with understanding and made to unbutton his kilt. I stopped him. "Wait. Let me have that honor."

He closed his eyes and nodded. I stood and walked around the fire, feeling its warmth diminish, as I grew closer to the realization of my own heated fantasy. The heady musk of his masculine body assailed my nostrils, and I felt blood surge into my nether regions. My hands shook as I raised them to slowly caress the muscular, hairy pecs, then slide through luxurious fur over six-pack abs and to the waistband of the tattered kilt. Willie's breath came slowly, but he never opened his eyes.

My questing fingers found the flap and crept under. An expanse of rough fabric grazed my fingertips, heightening their sensitivity until the roughness gave way to the warmth and suppleness of naked flesh. Willie's cock flexed as my fingers stroked its length, then wrapped around the thick, heavy stalk. He was growing turgid. He opened his eyes and looked at me but said nothing. I squeezed the growing member, slipping down to pinch the puckered foreskin. I was rewarded by a dollop of sticky fluid. I removed my hand and brought my fingers to my lips, licking the stickiness from them.

I had to have it. Dropping to my knees, between the crackling fire and the burly Highland god before me, I lifted the kilt and ducked my head under it. Instantly I was enveloped by the smell of sweat and sex. His sex. The growing cock brushed my cheek as I buried my nose in his bushy ball sac. They hung low and heavy, responding to my ministrations by jerking upward spasmodically. I inhaled deeply, then flicked the soft skin with my tongue. Somewhere above me, Willie groaned. I smiled and began licking at the hirsute testicles in earnest until they were soggy with my saliva.

By now the erection I'd been hoping for had become a reality. I pulled my head out from under the kilt and, with a flick of two fingers, unbuttoned the waistband. The kilt unfolded and slipped away, leaving Willie shivering in the night, his enormous cock bouncing stiffly now that it had been freed from the confines of the heavy cloth. The foreskin had rolled back just enough to reveal the tip of a purple head. Fluid oozed from the exposed piss slit. I sat back on my heels to take it all in.

Willie's cock was huge, nine inches long, I figured, but thicker than any I had ever encountered. I would be hard pressed to get an entire hand around its girth. Veins encircled it: large, pumping veins. Puckered flesh bunched around the tip, unraveling slowly as I pulled it back to reveal the angry head beneath. It was both the ugliest and most beautiful cock I had ever seen and I wanted more. I licked the precum from its slit and Willie's knees buckled slightly.

"Not here," he whispered coarsely. "Inside."

I nodded and watched as he turned and walked toward the mythical shack which, to my knowledge, no human eyes except those of Willie himself had ever borne witness to: the place that had once been described as "outside all laws of man and god." My eyes lingered on the hairy slabs of Willie's butt as they flexed with the exertion of his stride. He stopped at the door and turned toward me.

"Yew comin'?"

I nodded. He turned and pushed the door open, then stepped through into the darkness beyond. I stood and followed.

Once inside the shack, I was struck by how expansive it seemed. From the outside it seemed barely large enough to hold a few tools and maybe a man while standing upright. I had often wondered how Willie could sleep in what seemed like little more than a freestanding closet. I could see now that I'd been mistaken. The shack was large enough to be comfortable for one man. Sharpened tools hung menacingly from every wall. A roughly hewn table sat smack in the middle, covered with tools, rags and cleaning supplies. Beyond that was a tattered mattress pushed up against the far wall, lending a semblance of comfort to the sparse surroundings.

Willie stepped around the table, kicked a tangle of blankets aside and squatted before the mattress. Without turning, he asked, "Will this do?"

"It's perfect."

He nodded and crawled onto the mattress, rolling onto his back to stare at the ceiling. I followed, lowering myself down between his hairy legs and returning to my ministrations upon his crotch. His cock was still rock hard, and he sighed again as I slipped the foreskin back. A dark smell caressed my nostrils as I wrapped my lips around the head, sliding down to take it all in. My mouth barely accommodated it. There would be no way I would be able to engulf the shaft, too. Using my hand, I rolled the loose skin up and down along the shaft while licking and sucking at the head.

I don't know how long I'd been attacking the mythical cock with relish, but it was sopping wet from engorged tip to lathered balls when Willie groaned and began to pump feverishly upward.

"Whoa, Nelly," I said, backing away. "I'm not ready for you to blow just yet, old man."

Willie groaned again. "So, it's torture yer after then."

"Hardly," I responded, standing and quickly shucking off my own clothes until I was as naked as Willie in the shivering darkness of the shack. Willie looked confused. I turned and ran my hands over the smooth, moon-bright globes of my ass. "Your Fergie had an ass like this, Willie," I whispered.

His breathing grew brisk again. I squatted down beside him and waited until rough hands first cupped, then roughly caressed my ass.

"Would you like to come inside?" I asked. "Would you like to feel what I felt when I made love to her? Would you like to make love to her...through me?"

"Yew talk too much, boyo," the Scot groused gruffly.

Taking that as an answer in the affirmative, I turned and straddled Willie, stopping when his engorged head grazed the crack of my ass. I reached back and spread my cheeks wide, then rubbed my soon to be stretched hole across it. Precum oozed out to lubricate both. Willie was ready. I just hoped I was.

Taking a deep breath and letting it out slowly, I situated my asshole over his cock and pushed down. Willie's rough hands grasped my hips and his own rose up to meet them. There was a moment of stretching, followed by momentary pain, and the purple plum of his cockhead popped inside. I took another deep breath, blew it out and surged downward. Willie's breathing quickened. He pushed upward and I almost screamed. Before I knew it the entire length of his shaft had penetrated me. I felt lightheaded and couldn't catch my breath.

Willie, on the other hand, was encouraged. Using his hands to lift me up by my hips, he slammed me down onto his shaft, then did it a second and third time.

"Whoa, whoa, whoa…" I cautioned. "You're gonna split me in half. Slower. Slower!"

One of Willie's hands shot up and grabbed my face hard. My eyes popped open to find him staring maniacally up at me. "Yew've gone where no man has gone before, boyo! Yew wanted this, now yer gonna get it. All of it. All that Willie has to offer and more!"

I barely had time to register the threat when suddenly Willie grasped me like an expert wrestler, and with a twist and a roll I was on my back with the Highlander heavy upon me. His acrid breath was in my face as he settled into the new position. My ass screamed and the sound worked its way up to my mouth. A calloused hand squelched the scream as soon as it emerged, and Willie began pumping roughly into me like a wild, otherworldly beast.

"Yew want to be my Fergie?" he huffed. "She got away once by clocking me on the noggin with a haggis press. Willie had forgotten all about that, until now. Until yew awakened the memories with yer base desires. Yew want to experience love the way Willie would give it to that scheming, faithless bitch? To all of the faithless bitches who rejected him? Enjoy it while it lasts, boyo. Enjoy it while it lasts!"

Willie's breath came quicker and quicker, and his pumping increased until he was jackhammering my aching asshole like a piston machine. Smashing into my internal organs like a plundering Gaulish invader. As he grew closer and closer to orgasm, his hands wrapped around my throat and he began to squeeze.

"Feel me!" Willie shouted. "Feel my love, Fergie! Yew got away once, but yew'll nay get away again!"

I stared up into the face of my fantasy in realization and horror, trying desperately to breathe through constricted airways. His obsessions with the Aberdeen Strangler and the Duchess of York weren't just quirky fascination on his part. Why had nobody ever questioned the mysterious past of Groundskeeper Willie? Why had nobody ever probed the demons that haunted him? Why had nobody ever put two and two together?

My vision began to swim and the world around me to telescope outward. I was drowning. I was being sucked down into a thick, swirling void until even the pain wasn't registering anymore. The last thing my dimming eyes saw was the beast awakening fully as Willie howled and pumped his hot murderous essence deep into my bowels. Then, predictably, there was only darkness.

# OUT ON A LIMB

## William Holden

I stood back from the large picture window that overlooked my backyard hoping they couldn't see me. I was flushed with embarrassment. My skin was damp from the heat of the day and the mass of nerves that had invaded my body only moments ago. I had done it again. I had overcompensated for the fact that my body doesn't speak the same language as most people's, especially around good-looking men. My body becomes clumsy, awkward, and that's usually preceded by words spewing from my mouth with no discernable meaning. Today's fiasco was worse than normal. Today, there were two of them, two men, standing in front of me hot and sweaty from their work. All of which added up to me making a complete ass of myself.

They had arrived earlier than expected. A freak storm had hit the city less than a week ago and had left its heavy handprint in uprooted trees and downed power lines. I had been one of the more fortunate ones. My trees were for the most part intact, except for one: a seventy-year-old pine tree that towered over one hundred feet in my backyard. It had put up a good fight against the wind, but eventually it gave in and let the wind snap and twist many of its older, larger limbs. Unfortunately for them, the limbs that needed to come down were near the top.

I had just gotten out of the shower when I heard a knock at the front door. I quickly wrapped a towel around my waist and reached for my glasses. My vision blurred as I squinted through the steam-covered lenses. I found my way to the door and opened it. Dana, the arborist who had done some work for me in the past, stood on the other side of the storm door, but this time he wasn't alone. Modesty and my shyness took over. I crossed my chest with my arm as if that would somehow disguise my current state of undress.

"Alex, I'm sorry to catch you off guard like this." Dana gave the other man a brief smile. "It's good to see you again, although I'm not use to seeing you quite like this." He reached out and shook my hand. "This is Ian. He normally doesn't work this area, but with the recent storm, the company insisted that we double up." I accepted Ian's hand as Dana continued the introductions. "You called about some damage to one of your trees?"

"Yes. I'm sorry, please come in." I took a step back to open the door and slipped on the puddle that had formed beneath me on the hardwood floors. My grip on the doorknob held me up. "I don't usually answer the door like this." My face flushed as I noticed them staring at me. "I wasn't expecting you so soon."

"Yeah, we're sorry about that; the last job didn't take as long as we thought it would," Dana paused. "Hang on a second." He reached up and took the glasses off my face. "I don't see how you can see anything out of these." He slipped the glasses underneath the edge of his dark blue polo shirt to wipe the steam off of them. "There that should be better." He slipped them back on my face.

"Thanks." My eyes blinked as they refocused through the clear lenses. "If you don't mind, I think I'll get dressed. You can stay in here where it's air-conditioned or head around to the deck on the back of the house to take a look at the tree."

"There's no need for that; we saw the tree over the roofline when we pulled up," Ian responded. "It's going to be a bigger job than we thought."

"I'll go out to the trucks and start gathering up the ropes and saddles." Dana moved toward the door. "Give me a few minutes and I'll meet you both around back." He closed the door behind him, leaving Ian staring at me.

"Excuse me." I slid my glasses back up the bridge of my nose and headed down the hallway to the bedroom. I stopped long enough to grab a pair of underwear out of the top dresser drawer and then headed into the bathroom to finish getting ready.

I stood for a moment in front of the mirror looking at myself. My dirty blond hair was now mostly dry and looked as if it hadn't been combed in months. I tried to smooth it out but eventually gave up. I was applying deodorant to my second armpit when I felt as if I was being watched. I turned around with my right arm still in the air and saw Ian leaning against the frame of my bedroom door.

"Please, don't let me stop you."

"I...I didn't realize anyone was there," my voice wavered. I became aroused as he watched my morning grooming routine. He was sexy in an unassuming way. He stood an inch or two taller than me, five-ten perhaps, with a body that was well developed, yet not too extremely muscled. His dirty-blond hair was cut short and spiked on top. It was thinning even though he only looked to be in his late twenties. He had deep green eyes that were set against his smooth, almost childlike features. His elongated nose was narrow and curved slightly upward at the tip. His lips were thin with a rosy color to them. I could feel my dick stiffen under the towel. I turned away so he would notice.

I grabbed my underwear and tried to slip them on while still wearing the towel. I could feel him watching me, waiting for the towel to fall. I wanted nothing more than to have the balls to let the towel drop, to expose myself to him. I stumbled a few times and could feel the towel slipping. I lost my nerve and quickly shut the bathroom door.

I stood behind the closed door with the towel removed and wondered if he was still there. It was obvious what he had wanted, but that was always the problem. I had never developed the gay social skills. I was too shy to play the games, and if someone wanted to play I'd get nervous and leave before the first move was finished. I opened the door, expecting him to be standing there. The room was empty. I pulled on my jeans and T-shirt that I had laid out on my bed and headed down the hallway to the living room.

I stood at the large window and watched as they geared themselves up. The saddles hugged their waists with a thick leather strap. There were several nylon cords that hung off their legs and crotches. They wrapped their legs with the straps and then pulled another heavy nylon cord through their legs, fastening all of them together with large metal clasps. As they pulled and tightened their gear, the straps accented the shape of their crotches—they both appeared well-equipped in that area as well.

Both Ian and Dana were good looking but on opposite ends of the spectrum. Dana, unlike Ian, had more masculine and rugged features. His dark complexion was rough in appearance and covered with thick, black whiskers. His black hair was cut short and scattered with flecks of gray. He stood over six feet with broad shoulders and large sculpted arms.

Ian attached himself to the rope that Dana had lassoed around a large branch. Dana pulled and tugged on the rope and hoisted Ian off the ground till he reached the lowest limb to steady himself. A power saw hung from a metal clasp around Ian's waist. The bright orange electric cord fell to the ground near Dana's feet. Ian pulled himself up on the first large limb, studied the layout of the tree above him and then continued his climb. Soon Ian was out of sight; the only proof he was up there was the sway of the rope and the occasional pinecone falling to the ground.

My body jumped as the sudden sound of Ian's chainsaw buzzed to life. Sawdust filled the heavy, humid air and fell around Dana like some strange snowfall. The buzzing stopped, a crack echoed through the closed window, then a large branch came crashing to the ground with a heavy thud that shook the house. The rope that was tied to Ian began to sway. He was moving again. The chainsaw bit through the air, followed by more sawdust and another crack.

Dana grasped the rope to steady it. I could tell Ian was making his way back down. I walked to the refrigerator and pulled out several bottles of spring water. By the time I had reached Dana, Ian was halfway down the tree.

"I thought you could use something to cool you off." I handed him the bottle.

"Thanks." He twisted off the cap and took a long, slow drink. The heat and humidity of the day gave him a thick, musky scent. Sawdust stuck to his skin from the heavy layer of sweat. I watched the movement of his throat and large Adam's apple as he swallowed the ice-cold water.

"Where's mine?" Ian asked from behind me as he untied himself from the rope.

I handed him his own bottle and took in a deep breath of his own, sweet scent as he walked past me.

"Nice job," Dana commented as he took another drink.

"Yeah, it's going okay. I just wish it wasn't so fucking hot."

"Isn't it?" The words tumbled from my mouth before I could stop them. They both looked at me and smiled. An uneasy silence fell between us. Ian unscrewed the bottle cap and took a small sip of the water.

"That's perfect." Ian set the bottle down on the ground and grabbed the edge of his polo shirt and pulled it up over his head. He wore a white T-shirt underneath. The thin material, threadbare in spots, torn in others, had seen better days. A dark circle of sweat stained the fabric under each arm. He bent down and picked up the bottle. It was covered in sweat of its own.

My heart began to pound in my chest as I watched Ian lift the bottle and pour the cold liquid over his head. It trailed down his face and neck and soaked his T-shirt. I could see his large, dark nipples slowly appear through the wet fabric and the scattering of damp chest hair between his pecs.

"You're unbelievable." Dana half laughed. "We've got other clients to go to once we're done here and look at you."

"I don't know," I spoke up, determined more than ever to play the game. "I think he's got the right idea." I took my bottle of water and poured it over my head. I let out a brief scream as the intense cold bit at my overheated skin. I quickly dropped the bottle on the ground and began to pull my T-shirt over my head. My pulse, driven by my dick, was racing with a boldness I had never known before. I then began to panic as I realized my arms and head were stuck in the T-shirt. I wiggled and tugged on the material as the wet fabric clung heavily to my damp skin. I could hear Ian and Dana laughing. I felt the material give. I pulled on the edge of the T-shirt with every ounce of scrawny muscle I had.

My head popped out and I went tumbling to the ground.

I lay there for a moment in disbelief, my body covered in pine needles and sawdust. Ian and Dana seemed to tower over me as they laughed and clapped each other on the shoulders. My glasses had been pulled off in the struggle. I frantically scanned the ground and saw the glimmer of the lenses in the morning sun. I placed them on my face as I stood up. I brushed myself off and ran into the house, mortified with how my bold move had gone.

I tossed the shirt on the floor and walked closer to the window, partially hiding myself with the drapes. Ian and Dana were talking, but their voices were muted. Dana pointed in the direction of the house. I ducked my head behind the curtain so they wouldn't see me watching them. I decided I didn't want to see them talking about me, so I headed into the bathroom to clean myself up.

I turned on the water and ran the bar of soap through my hands to work up a good lather. I closed my eyes and rubbed the soap over my face and neck. Leaning over the sink, I threw several handfuls of water onto my face to rinse. Blindly, I reached for the hand towel to dry my face.

"Are you looking for this?" Ian's voice startled me. He placed the hand towel in my outstretched hand.

I stood up from my bent position and turned off the water. "Thanks." I opened my eyes. He stood with his arms above his head, leaning in the doorway. His dirt-covered T-shirt was pulled up above his waist. I could see the frayed edge of the waistband of his underwear. My eyes moved away and caught the long dark hairs of his armpits poking out of the sleeves of his T-shirt. His blue polo shirt hung from one of the loops of his saddle. I tried not to stare, but I wanted desperately to burn the image of him in my mind; to store it in my memory for recall when I needed private inspiration.

"Don't mention it." His body swung in and out of the doorway in a seductive dance. He noticed my attention to his body and smiled. "Are you okay, I mean, you know, after your fall?" He tried to hold in a brief laugh but couldn't.

"I'm fine, so if you're done laughing at me you can head back outside to finish what I'm paying you for." The tone of my voice came out harsher then I had expected.

"Look, I'm sorry." He walked up to me. "I really did come to see if you were okay. You took a nasty fall."

"I'm fine." I backed away from his closeness and found myself pressed against the vanity. I had nowhere else to go. He moved in closer. I could feel the heat of his body surround me. His scent, woody and thick, drifted into my nose. I took another breath of him. My body trembled with nerves and desire. My cock stirred restlessly in my pants. His seductive eyes, voice and body engulfed me.

"You are so adorable when you're nervous."

"I'm not nervous." The tremble in my voice told another story.

"No? Your eye is twitching and I can hear your heart pounding from here." Ian leaned back slightly, gripped the bottom of his T-shirt and slowly pulled it up.

My eyes followed every inch of his exposed skin. His firm stomach appeared silky smooth except for a thin trail of light brown hair that led down from his navel and into his jeans. My eyes continued to follow the edge of his shirt as my anticipation and desire grew. The dark rounds of his nipples stood out against his light skin and firm chest. A scattering of dirty-blond hair lay damp between them. The scent of his sweat mixed with the metallic undertones of his deodorant became stronger as the material lifted away from his armpits. The dark brown hair under his arms stuck to his skin, in thick, wet curls. He dropped the shirt on the floor and leaned against me, placing his arms on either side of my body.

"Do you want me to stop?" His cheek rubbed against mine as he whispered in my ear.

"No, but..."

"But what?" He kissed my neck.

"What about Dana?" His sweat dampened body clung to my skin as he pressed his body against mine.

"Dana's too into his job to worry about us. He'll be in that tree for hours."

"But..." He kissed my neck again, then my throat, my chin, until his lips met mine, cutting off my words. His tongue, thick and meaty, entered my mouth. Bittersweetness flooded my taste buds. His hands grabbed my waist. I felt my body rise off the floor as he lifted me and set me down on the counter. He pulled my hips to the edge. I could feel the solid mass of his cock pressing into me. I threw my head back against the wall as he moved back down my neck. His tongue and lips ignited nerve endings I never knew existed as they licked and nibbled the small nubs of my nipples.

His mouth moved farther down my body, licking the salty sweat that lingered on my skin. I felt his hands move up my legs. His fingers found the head of my cock and rubbed it through the thick denim. My cock expanded from his touch and expelled a river of precome that soaked through the material. My body shivered from head to toe as his mouth descended on my stomach. His tongue ran along the edge of my pants, leaving a trail of his spit against my skin. His hands quickly undid my belt, button and zipper.

Ian stood back and pulled my jeans and underwear off. I

kicked them to the floor. My erect cock fell against my stomach with a wet smack. I wrapped my legs around his body and pulled him into me. He smiled at my sudden aggressiveness before bending his head against my stomach and running his tongue in a tiny circle over the head of my cock. I arched my hips and slipped my cock into his mouth.

I fucked his mouth with heavy thrusts sending weeks of built-up precome into his waiting mouth. His hands were between us as he fumbled with the heavy metal clasps and nylon cords of his saddle.

"Shit," he grumbled as he pulled my cock out of his mouth, "these goddamn belts!"

"Fuck the belt." I pulled his mouth onto mine and tasted my own precome lingering on his tongue. I reached down and unzipped his pants. My hand, much smaller than his, fit easily inside the fly. His moans vibrated down my throat as my hand wrapped around his wet cock. Its short, thick shaft fit nicely in my hand. I pulled it out and rubbed the excess precome over my ass.

Ian looked at me as I fingered myself, first one, then two. He bit his lower lip as if anticipating an expensive meal after a long fast. I reached down and guided his cock to my ass. I felt the head of it pushing into me. A sharp, sudden pain rushed through me as Ian's cock pushed through the small opening of my ass. He paused and leaned into me. His stale breath beat against my face. My body shook as another inch of him entered me. I felt the pulse of his cock beating against the opening of my ass. I took a deep breath and relaxed as the remaining few inches slipped inside.

I looked at Ian and saw pleasure caressing his face as his cock settled into me. I tightened and released the muscles of my ass in rapid succession, milking his cock further. He groaned and brought my hips closer against him, sending a wave of electricity through my body. My legs were pushed farther down until my feet were planted against the wall over my head.

I felt his cock pulling out of me, slowly, deliberately. It stopped briefly before he slammed his hips back into me. I let out a quick yell as the painful pleasure of his cock invaded my ass once again. I reached out for something to support myself against his thrusts. I grabbed on to his saddle and wrapped my fingers around the metal clasps. Our bodies became a tangled mass spread out on the bathroom counter. Sweat dripped from Ian's face and neck and fell against my body. The straps of the saddle slapped the surface of the vanity with loud hollow thumps.

My face and neck were covered in my own precome as my cock hung erect over my face. My ass, sore from the width of Ian's cock, continued to receive his thrusts. I didn't want him to stop, no matter how sore I became, but I knew that neither of us could hold out much longer.

Ian's breath became heavy and labored as he continued to fuck me. I felt his cock swell inside of me. I imagined his come building within his swollen balls, waiting for the fine line to be crossed. He grabbed my cock and began stroking it in unison with his thrusts. I felt my own orgasm nearing the surface, burning, building as the pressure mounted behind it. Suddenly my face and mouth were flooded with the warmth of my own come. I opened my mouth wider and shot another load into it. Ian released my cock and let it dangle over me. Come leaked from the piss slit, swirling over my chest, neck and face with the force of Ian's thrusts. He pulled himself out of me and showered his come over my ass and balls. He rubbed himself between my legs and shot another thick load.

"Ian," a distant voice called. "Get your ass out here!"

"Shit." Ian pulled himself off of me. "Fuck, I lost track of time."

I stood up. My weak legs wanted to give out. I wobbled from my own weight and braced myself against the counter. My raw overworked ass burned. It felt good, like an old friend that had gone missing and then turned up. I smiled as I watched Ian force his limp cock back into his jeans.

"What's so funny?"

"Nothing, really. It's just this." I motioned with my hands at the scattering of clothes and the obvious state we were in.

"You're fucking adorable." He placed his hands against my cheeks and kissed me.

"Ian. Where the fuck are you?"

I stood naked, sore and covered in come and watched Ian run through the bedroom pulling his T-shirt over his head. I cleaned myself up as best as I could and headed outside to check on the job.

"You all done?"

"Just about. Can't stay around here all day and play," Dana replied. "We've got other clients to get to."

"Where's Ian?"

"I sent him on ahead to the next house while I finish cleaning up here." He stopped and looked at me. "You don't mind do you?"

"Why should I care? Look, I'm heading back into the house. When you're done out here and want the check come and get me." I stood waiting for some type of reply. His saddle still hung around his waist. The nylon cords dangled from his legs and crotch as he bent down to pick up his tools. Getting no response, I left him to finish his job.

I walked into my study and grabbed the checkbook. A pack of Marlboro cigarettes sat next to it. I pulled one out of the pack and headed to the back deck to smoke while I waited for Dana to finish. I lit the cigarette and took a long drag, enjoying the flavor and the aftereffects of the sex.

Dana came up from behind me. "That should do it." He took the cigarette from my hand and took a long drag on it. He looked at it and placed it between my lips. He exhaled. The smoke lingered around my face.

"Let me get you the check." I stepped on the cigarette and headed into the house with Dana behind me.

"Alex, do you think I could borrow your clothes dryer?"

"Sure, I guess."

"Thanks, I just want to try to dry some of the sweat out of my shirt before my next client. After all it's sort of your fault."

"My fault?" I led him back into the laundry room. "What's my fault?" I opened up the dryer and tossed in a few fabric sheets. He pulled off his polo shirt without hesitation or modesty and tossed it into the dryer. I shut the door and turned it on. The low hum of the dryer filled the room. "So what's my fault?"

"You really don't know?" He looked at me as he shut the door to the laundry room. The dryer slowly heated the air in the room. Dana's sweat filtered through the air and mixed with the scent of the fabric sheets. His body, dark bronze from days in the sun and covered in a thick blanket of curly black hair, teased my emotions. Sawdust and wood shavings clung in the tangles of his sweat-dampened hair. "You and Ian."

"What are you talking about?"

"Don't try to deny it. I saw everything while I was out on the limb. I could see right into the bathroom. I watched Ian fuck you."

"Shit." My face reddened with embarrassment.

"For two years, I've been coming here and nothing from you." He bent down and unlaced his tan work boots. "I've hinted around, made remarks, but nothing."

"I'm not good at picking up on signals," I said in my own defense.

"Well, you seemed to do quite well with Ian today."

"It wasn't like that. He didn't hint around; he just told me what he wanted."

"Well, now it's my turn to get what I want." He pulled off his tan work boots and tossed them to me. I caught one, but the other hit the floor with a heavy thud. The musky and masculine smell of his overheated foot poured out of the boot. My cock stretched as I took another deep breath of him.

He unbuttoned his jeans and fly in one quick tug. I could see the white ribbed underwear as his jeans fell open. The gray band of his Andrew Christian briefs ran across his firm, hairy stomach. He pulled his jeans down and then stood up, never once taking his eyes off of me. My heart pounded in my throat. I'd become frozen with disbelief since he confessed his secret desire. My entire body broke out in a cold sweat. The air had gotten hot in the enclosed room as the dryer continued to tumble.

Dana's cock stretched the thin fabric of his underwear. Precome soaked a large area where the tip of his cock lay. I could see the outline of the veins as they pressed against the damp fabric. He pulled his underwear down, and his cock stuck out in front of him. His large furry balls hung heavily between his legs. He stepped out of his pants and underwear, leaving himself naked except for the white socks on his feet. A smile appeared on his face as he approached me. The scent of his body filled the room with its potent perfume.

"What about your next client?"

He put a finger to my lips. "I don't want to talk. I'm here to get what's been coming to me." He replaced his finger with his lips. They were hot and covered in the day's sweat. He pushed me against the wall. His hands pressed firmly against my chest. I felt his tongue pushing its way into my mouth, and I opened for it.

My hands ran down his muscular back. A new layer of sweat from the heat of the room covered his skin. I reached farther down and felt a patch of hair where the crack of his ass began. My hands trembled as I slipped a finger down his wet, hair-covered crack. I squeezed his ass with my hands to spread his cheeks. I drew tiny circles around his tight hole and felt the muscles of his ass respond.

He pulled his lips off of mine. His eyes were steaming ovals of desire as they looked at me. He grabbed my T-shirt and ripped it open from the chest. The sudden force of his act startled and excited me. His hands cupped my chest and squeezed. His strength brought tears to my eyes as he pulled and pinched my erect nipples. He knelt down in front of me and ran his hand over the bulge in my jeans. His fingers worked quickly on the button and zipper, pulling my pants and underwear down the minute they were released. My cock fell against his face, smearing my precome over his cheek. He grabbed my cock at the base and ran his tongue over the head, licking the precome as it seeped out of the piss slit.

My knees became weak, and my legs shook as he took the full length of my cock in one swallow. I grabbed his head to support myself. My mind buzzed with a mass of emotions and desires. I closed my eyes to my surroundings and let the feel of his tongue and lips be my only concern. The pressure around my ass brought me out of my thoughts as he slipped a finger inside of me. I had reached my limit. I could feel the come burning inside of me. He could tell by the swelling of my cock in his mouth that I was getting close. He pulled my cock out of his mouth as I shot the first load. It landed on his cheek and clung to the dark stubble of his face. He stroked my cock hard. I showered his chest and neck with several thick loads of milky white come. He pumped and stroked my cock until every last drop had been released onto his body.

"Turn around." He stood up and pushed me against the wall. His finger slid back inside. He leaned into me. "Now it's my turn." He pulled his finger out and shoved his cock into my sore, overworked ass. He pressed his body against mine and began fucking me without any play or build-up.

His cock, thicker and longer than Ian's, filled my ass with pleasure. I reached behind me and wrapped my fingers around it as he pulled himself in and out of my ass. Ian's leftovers and Dana's precome mixed with the sweat-dampened hair around my ass. I could feel the hair clinging to his cock as he pushed farther and harder into me.

My cock bobbed up and down, swelling then going soft over and over as Dan's thrusts became more pronounced. Precome streamed from it and hung off the tip then released to the floor as the weight became too great. I could feel his cock swelling inside of me, the head drilling deeper into me as his breaths beat against my back. Dana brought his face to the back of my neck. His grunts and groans became muted by the sweat of our bodies, and then my ass suddenly filled with a flood of hot come.

He leaned back off my body and continued to fuck me harder and harder, sending more of his come into me. It filled me to capacity. As he pulled his cock out, I could feel come running down my legs. He slapped my ass hard. The sound of his hand against my wet asscheeks vibrated around us.

Dana already had his underwear back on as I turned around. He looked at me and winked. "I'm not bringing anyone with me the next time you need me to do some work for you. Oh, and when you make another appointment, call my direct line. That way they won't send someone else here to do my work for me." He pulled his shirt out of the dryer and sniffed around the armpits. "Thanks for this, too." He pulled his shirt over his head and motioned for me with his finger. I hesitated. "Get over here," he said with a smile. "You need to loosen up a bit, that's all. Just be yourself, clumsy or awkward, it's okay; just don't fight it." He kissed me then looked into my eyes. "Let's hope another storm blows in soon, or now that you have my direct line, just give me a call for whatever."

I watched him walk down my driveway and hop up into his work truck. As he pulled away, I grabbed the phone and dialed his number.

# SUMMER HEAT

A. C. Faro

The heat pressing in against the auto's glass and heady scent of new leather under my ass were making me hard. The reason was both simple and ironic. Despite being a guy who wrote about sex for a living, I hadn't had any in over two months. The stirring in my cargo shorts was just a sad, if not mocking, reminder of this fact.

Work was primarily to blame. I'd been busting my hump on a supernatural teleplay for the better part of a year, which a major cable channel mercifully purchased a few weeks ago. Its competition boasted a runaway hit show centered on dangerous, sex-starved vampires (were there any other kind?), and the underdog network was out for some serious commercial payback. I provided it in the form of *Incubus Nights*, a trashy yet compelling tale of studly Xander Lewis, an urban twenty-something who woke up one morning to find that he'd become a sex demon.

Imagine the possibilities.

Unlike most writers (read narcissists), I'd included nothing of autobiographical merit in *Incubus Nights*. Who was I to stroke my own ego by modeling a fictional hero after myself? It was pure coincidence that Xander and I both happened to be tall, blond, hot and packing large cocks. Okay. I may have embellished a bit there. I was an attractive thirtysomething sporting ten extra pounds, with a dick half a block north of seven inches, depending on your starting point.

At any rate, with the contract negotiations behind me and a juicy paycheck in the bank, I was exhausted, super horny, and in need of a complete writing-free getaway.

Longtime friends Justin and Riley had provided the perfect escape with an invitation to their new digs in Palm Springs.

The navigation system led me to what used to be a ramshackle midcentury modern. After eight grueling months of remodeling, however, my friends' *new* place resembled a home straight off the cover of *Architectural Digest*. I could hardly wait to see what the inside was like.

Then it happened.

From the Teutonic bliss of my A5, I tumbled into the farthest recesses of hell. A furnacelike blast of air assaulted me as soon as I opened the car door. Exiting, I had to stand still for a moment to allow a wave of dizziness to pass, and the mariachi music filtering over the stucco retaining wall was either a hallucination or Justin's musical tastes had radically changed since last we'd seen each other.

The music helped me to focus on something other than the debilitating heat, but by the time I reached the front door, my clothes were glued to me. This was Palm Springs in summer for godsakes, not Miami.

To my greater disappointment, it was nearly as sweltering inside and my friends were nowhere in sight. A cute Hispanic guy was. He glanced up from setting a floor tile into place as I closed the front door and regarded me with questioning eyes.

"*Hola. Soy Derrick.*" I had to shout over the blare of horns and hissing maracas. "*Un amigo de la...*" My Spanish sucked. "A friend of the owners."

He hit a button on the dusty boom box next to him and the music died away with a protracted echo. "They aren't here."

On the bright side, I could dispense with my atrocious Spanish.

Reaching into my pocket, I pulled out my cell phone to check it for messages. Nothing. Justin and Riley knew I was coming. It wasn't like them not to leave word for me.

The worker got up and lifted his T-shirt to wipe the band of perspiration from his forehead. The show of abs was impressive. "Aldo," he said, walking over to me with an extended hand and the beginnings of a smile. "They went to Home Depot. They should be back in an hour."

Nice firm shake. Nice firm everything.

Well, that explained the missing friends. In an attempt to come across as something less than lecherous, I decided to take in the sheer volume of the open-concept living, dining and family rooms. The place was massive. Except for drywall and the travertine flooring, though, not much else had gone in. The AC was clearly not up and running, which, *please god*, meant we'd be staying at the leased condo in Rancho Mirage over the weekend. "I'll just hang out here until they get back, if that's okay?"

"You bet. It's really hot out there."

*It's really hot in here, too*, I thought, giving his sexy, lean frame the once-over.

How amazing that I could be so uncomfortable and still reason with my dick. Nevertheless, two things had to occur before encouraging my libido (and possible embarrassment) any further. Oddly enough, the first happened to center on my dick: I had to piss. Slugging down a gallon of ice-cold water was second on the agenda. "Is there a bathroom I can use?"

He grinned, pointing at a doorway off the main entrance and giving me the same appraising look. "To the left and then down the hall. It's the only one hooked up."

"Thanks."

It was a super-tacky thing to do, but I couldn't help shrugging out of my damp T-shirt. The last few months of wrapping up the teleplay had left me anything but toned and tanned, and I had the pale, annoying beginnings of love handles to prove it.

My plans for the weekend would fix that. There was nothing like flopping by a pool by day and having great sex by night to help shed those unwanted pounds.

I tossed the T-shirt onto a stack of dark walnut shelves and then moved in the direction Aldo had indicated. How these men worked under such miserable conditions and with all their clothes on, I hadn't a clue. The decrepit swamp cooler chugging away in the other room only pushed the warm, humid air around in circles. Though I had to admit, the airflow against my naked skin did feel pretty damned good. And this part of the house, which had to be the master suite, was slightly cooler and fresher than the main living space.

The mariachi music kicked back in while I navigated the maze of rooms. The place was fifty-six-hundred square feet. I lived in less than a thousand.

Justin and Riley clearly enjoyed their space.

When the labyrinth ended at the master bathroom, I stumbled upon a hunky Minotaur lording over a grout sponge and some spectacular wall tile. Didn't my friends hire any unattractive workers?

"What up?" he said, cocking his head and eyeballing me over his shoulder.

Common courtesy dictated I stop staring. Something told me that this stud was accustomed to people ogling him. Sex appeal oozed from every pore. His back and shoulder muscles stretched the fabric of his T-shirt to its limits; his ass showed two solid mounds beneath the stained khaki work pants. Above all, his striking youthful face sealed the deal. Urination and heatstroke be damned. Blood was pumping fast and furiously into my groin, my cock inching down the leg of my cargo shorts for the second time today.

"Sorry. I, uh, need to use the toilet."

He turned around, dropping the sponge into a bucket of grayish water at his feet; a cool reserve reflected in his eyes—or was it appraisal? His thick, black hair was cut close to the scalp, but high cheekbones, elongated eyes, and a more reddish skin tone spoke of Native American ancestry. His broad shoulders and chest tapered to a slim waist and hips, and while he matched my six-two frame for height, everything else about him was exotic in comparison to my more conventional Irish features.

I followed his dark eyes down to my obvious erection. "Looks like," he said, the tone neither friendly nor aloof. "Gonna go grab some water. Take your time, man."

When he moved past, I got a whiff of musky scent. It screamed of the sweaty, tumble-between-the-sheets kind of sex you wanted to bury your nose in and taste.

The business end of *Incubus Nights* may have robbed me of my horniness, but I was primed to get it back. And nothing would bring it home sooner than pounding the tight ass of a hot guy.

Too bad this one didn't seem interested.

Then again, being straight might have something to do with

it. My SDR (Straight Dude Radar) was clanging like a four-alarm fire bell inside my head.

Self-conscious and frustrated, I exhaled deeply and approached the toilet, lifting up the lid and pulling out my rock-hard dick. I couldn't piss until it softened up, and there were only two things to do about that: stand there like an idiot and wait, or jerk my bad boy off.

Wound this tightly, I could probably bust a nut fast enough that no one would ever be the wiser. Option two it was.

A sulky glance over my shoulder assured me that I was alone. Still, I fantasized that my hunky Indian stud was standing behind me, his own hard-on out for viewing. With no lube around, I had to be content with the gob of saliva I'd spit onto my knob, which I began to slide up and down the length of my shaft. It felt so fucking good. I closed my eyes and pumped a little harder, legs bent slightly, my quads tensing up.

Oh, yeah, it wouldn't take long to pop off a nice load. I used my free hand to tease and pinch my nipples. That would get me off in a heartbeat.

"Hey, I thought you needed to piss?"

I froze in mid-stroke. The Indian was staring over at me, the reflection in his dark brown, almost black, eyes anything but hostile.

"This a solo thing?" he said, rubbing the fly of his khakis. "Or can anyone party?"

He didn't wait for a response before yanking off his T-shirt, which he tossed onto the floor. The man had the smoothest, bronze-colored skin and flattest stomach I'd ever seen. His pecs were perfection—not the bloated, steroid half-moons so popular with gym rats. Chiseled and squared beneath dark nipples, they caused my cock to twitch in my hand, my tongue involuntarily to lick across my lower lip. Work pants and underwear soon went the way of his T-shirt, his semierect prick swinging low and meaty. It had to be monstrous when hard.

*All the better to play with while I fuck the shit out of you.*

"The party's right here," I said, stepping out of my shorts and kicking them aside. I walked over to him and glanced down at my cock. "Get it started."

With narrowed eyes, he shook his head. "Got a better idea. You come make friends with mine instead. Bet you ain't never had no Cahuilla meat in your mouth before."

Two alphas in the same doghouse.

This was gonna be interesting.

I moved closer, the head of my dick poking the base of his, precome snailing a trail into his pubes. I leaned in to kiss his full lips but he turned away.

Yup. Straight.

I dropped to my knees to give him what he wanted, lifting the arrow-shaped head of that pendulous cock with my tongue. I tugged it into my mouth and began nursing the spongy shaft, licking and teasing the sheathed head until it came out of hiding. At the rate his flesh was swelling, I wasn't sure I'd be able to blow him much longer. He was *that* big.

He leaned against the wall with a throaty groan, hands on the back of my head urging me to go deeper. His hips joined the mouth-fucking party with firm, rhythmic thrusts. "Suck it!" he growled, making me gag on it, spit dribbling out the corners of my mouth. "You like that shit, don'tcha?"

I used some of the excess saliva to pump my meat, sweat rolling down my sides and back and funneling into my asscrack, while he continued to power-slam my tonsils. I was always the aggressor during sex. Letting someone else take that control was a new experience. It was also damned hot.

"Get ready," he said, arching over my back and slapping my

left buttcheek. "Papi's gonna split that real good."

The force from his slap sent a not-so-unpleasant sting of heat coursing through my body. Then he jammed a finger in my virgin hole and began working it in and out. My body jerked and then froze in response. Giving up *that* much control might be too much to ask.

Besides, my talents were better served when I was in the driver's seat.

I pulled off his dick and stood up, his finger popping out of my hole. "I don't get fucked."

He stared at me as if I were joking. *Mr. Stud* was no doubt used to getting his way with the ladies. I had my boundaries, and that put us at an impasse.

"And I don't kiss guys," he hit back, reaching down into the pile of clothes on the floor. He stood up with a condom and sample-sized tube of lube. Talk about being prepared.

For a second, I thought things might turn ugly. I'd made myself clear; I didn't take it up the ass. But then he surprised me by saying, "So how 'bout a compromise?"

He bridged the distance, and then our sweaty chests were rubbing and sliding over each other, our cocks playing dueling swords. Then he shocked me by pressing those full lips against mine, brushing his tongue along the opening. They were so soft, his breath so inviting, like cool water to a dying man in the desert. And I had no problem drinking from that well.

We worked each other up again, his kisses hungry and eager now. He held me to him with a powerful arm, a corner of the condom's wrapper between his fingers poking at my lower back. He bent at the knees, twisting some and allowing me to control our kissing. He reached between my legs, around my cock and under my balls, his middle finger finding my warm, moist hole, which he teased and then entered.

The sensation this time was decidedly different. He'd found my G-spot and worked it with uninhibited abandon. "Fucking hell!" I gasped, as a surprise rope of white cum shot out the head of my dick and caught him on the chin. "Keep doing that!"

"Count on it," he growled.

Before I knew what was happening, he had the condom rolled onto the length of his fat prick and was turning me around. I braced forearms against the cool, dusty tile and thrilled at the suction his chest and stomach made against the hot, sweaty skin of my back. He pushed my legs farther apart with a knee and nudged the first inch of himself against my puckering hole.

I started to say, *Take it easy*, when I felt him breach me, but he slid inside as though I were a pro at taking cock, which did not stop me from letting out a loud groan. It also did not stop the electric current of pain shooting through my entire body.

Nonetheless, I wouldn't have asked him to take it out for the world. "Fuck me harder," I demanded, slapping a palm against the tile. "C'mon, man!"

An arm hooked around my waist, the other braced against the nape of my neck, and then he did exactly what I asked him to—and then some. I marveled at how it could hurt so bad and yet feel so fucking great as he bucked and thrust against me, balls slapping against the sensitive ridge between my anus and nut sac and giving me a double prostate massage.

We'd been going at it for some time when he turned us, lowering me to the floor, his cock never leaving my ass; then he positioned me on hands and knees and the real pounding began.

My grunts and moans echoed throughout the bathroom. Even the mariachi music seemed to pale in comparison.

"Hey, leave some of that for me, Jose," I heard a familiar voice say.

I opened my eyes to see Aldo standing in the doorway. He shared a secret smile with my Indian stud and then let his pants drop. His body may have been lean, but there was nothing spare about his beautiful dick, which he wasted no time stuffing into my mouth.

"So…fucking…tight," Jose said between gritted teeth, slamming my ass even harder. "He's gonna make me blow."

"Wait for me," Aldo said and then began face-fucking me with uniform gusto.

Sweat poured from our naked bodies, my eyes stinging from the salty droplets, but that didn't stop me from sucking him faster or pushing my hungry ass farther onto Jose's ruthless cock. I managed to brace myself on one forearm and jerk off with my free hand. I was getting damned close myself, then Jose and Aldo found the perfect rhythm. I matched my strokes to theirs, the bathroom damp and ripe with the smell of male sex, our grunts and moans echoing around us, inciting us toward one helluva release, for which we didn't have to wait long.

Aldo let loose first.

His entire body shook as he sent the first jet of warm spunk shooting against the back of my throat. It seemed endless, the jerky, jabbing thrusts followed by more jism flooding my mouth. I took it all into me with greedy satisfaction and then began to shudder at the same moment Jose did. He gripped the sides of my ass and squeezed hard, snarling as he drove the length of himself into me one last, violent time. The movement pushed me over the edge, and I fired off a load with such force that it landed on Aldo's upper thighs.

He pulled back, his hard dick popping out of my mouth, and laughed. "Damn!"

Jose fell forward, his sweat-soaked belly making sucking noises against my back as he shuddered and breathed heavily.

"Knew you had it in you."

"Hello?" It was Justin's voice from the living room. "Where are you guys?"

Three men never scrambled into clothes so quickly. By some miracle, when Justin and Riley appeared in the open doorway, we were dressed, if not a bit sweaty and overheated.

"So what do you think?" Justin asked with a grin, indicating Aldo, Jose and the bathroom around us, oblivious to what had just happened. "Amazing, aren't they?"

I smirked over at my new friends and then back at Justin and Riley. "And then some."

"It's wicked hot in here," Riley said, moving over to the exterior glass door and opening it. "And that grout sealer smells funky."

I was hoping to smell more of it later that night.

# RISKY SEX

## Bob Vickery

It's a little after eleven o'clock, late enough to draw a decent bar crowd, but early enough, if I'm lucky, to score and still catch a few hours' sleep. I have to be in the hiring hall by eight o'clock sharp tomorrow morning if I'm to get a crack at a job. It's crazy to be cruising on a weekday night, but I haven't been laid since I've moved out here and my cock is giving me a hard time about it. Springsteen is playing on the jukebox, and the boys are lined up against the walls, checking out any new action that walks through the door. I feel their eyes draw a bead on me, and it's gratifying to see how they track me as I push my way through the crowd. I need a little tender loving tonight; I'm feeling lonely and more than a little depressed about not finding work.

I make my way to the bar and order the cheapest beer they got, which is still three goddamn dollars. As I pull the bills from my wallet, I realize that I'm going to have to nurse this sucker for the rest of the night. That is, unless I can get someone to buy me another. This is very possible. I'm muscular and hairy, with the face of a back-alley thug, perfect fodder for all those guys out there with fantasies of getting it on with a knuckle-dragger. And they *are* out there. I found out long ago that by just leaning against a wall and looking stupid, I can usually draw in someone looking for a little walk on the wild side.

Within half an hour I've hooked up with a couple of boyfriends with a place in the Village. One's a humpy little dago with a tight compact body and dark soulful eyes. He tells me his name is Lou, short for Luigi. His buddy is lighter, with blond hair, a kid's face, and the tall, lean body of a competitive swimmer. They both fall into the "sex candy" category, and I'm quite happy to be their stray mutt for the night. We talk the usual barroom bullshit, and I answer their questions as politely as I'm capable of, waiting for them to make up their minds. When the blond guy, whose name is Charley, asks me what I do for a living, I tell him I'm an iron man. Well, that tips the scales in my balance fast enough; I can see they're about to cream in their jeans at the thought of making it with a *construction worker.* They exchange glances, raise their eyebrows and give each other a silent nod, with all the subtlety of a two-by-four between the eyes. It's funny, but they seem to think I'm too clueless to notice any of this. Or else they just don't care. They finally ask if I want to go home with them and I say, "Sure."

Riding in their car, I pick up signals that these guys want someone mean and stupid. I think about calling this off but decide to just go ahead and play the game. When we get back to their place, I throw them around the bedroom, rough them up a bit, rip their clothes off, and then make them strip me naked. Lou pulls my pants down; when my dick springs out to full attention he looks like a kid who just got a new bike for Christmas. I grab his head and start fucking his face hard while Charley eats out my ass. Lou is no slouch at giving head. I close my eyes and let the sensations sweep over me of having my dick *finally* in some place warm and wet. We play out all the expected riffs on the theme of the big, bad construction worker. I call them "faggots" and "cocksuckers" and knock them around some more. But later on, I let them turn the tables on me. Charley pins *me* down as Lou slowly works a greased dildo up my ass. I snarl and spit, cursing threats at them, with all of us just having a grand old time. I end up fucking them both in retaliation, first Lou, then Charley, then Lou again, because I find him the hotter of the two. I shoot my load while plowing him, and as I squirt it deep into the condom up his ass, I throw back my head and bellow like a bull. A neighbor pounds on the wall and shouts at us to shut the fuck up. I lie back while Lou and Charley kneel over me and shoot on my face. They beg me to spend the night, but I tell them no, I got plans tomorrow morning. When they don't give it up, I kick over an end table and tell them to go fuck themselves. They love it.

On the subway back I think about how easy it was to give them what they wanted. Hell, if things get desperate enough, I could always try hustling. Christ, I hope it doesn't come to that.

I luck out. The next morning I finally land a job up on Lexington Avenue. One of the iron men there took a flop yesterday and fell two stories, breaking his leg. Tough luck for him. Lucky break for me. Oh, does that sound callous? Excuse me; I'll be more sensitive when I have more than fifty-seven bucks in my checking account.

I show up the next day right at eight o'clock, like I was told to; I'm not about to do anything to blow this gig. The building's a big motherfucker all right, already fifty-four stories worth of iron thrown up, with another twenty-two to go. I take the lift up to where the crew is punching in. By force of habit, I zero in on the humpiest guy there, some Irish piece of tail with a red crew cut, alert blue eyes and a tight, sexy body that's just screaming for a serious plowing. I ask him what the foreman's name is and where I can find him.

He gives me a quick look over. "His name's Jackson," he says. "Last I saw him, he was over by the derrick bull wheel."

"What does he look like?"

He gives a hint of a smile. "Think pit bull on steroids." He buckles on his tool belt and hoists a coil of cable onto his shoulder. "Just go over there. You can't miss him."

It doesn't take long to find Jackson. The guy was right. He does have the small bloodshot eyes and sloped head of an attack dog. I report in, and he looks me over, his eyes pausing for a second on the four gold rings pierced in my left ear. He doesn't look too happy with what the cat drug in. We're standing just a few feet away from the bull wheel and have to shout to hear each other. "The hall tells me you're a connector," he growls. "Is that for real?"

I nod. "For five years. Out in L.A."

Jackson squints his eyes, a third-rate Clint Eastwood. "Oh, yeah? Why'd you come out here?"

*What,* I think. *I need a passport?* But I know how crews guard their turfs like junkyard dogs. I give my best shit-eating smile. "Construction's gone to hell out West. All the trades are scrambling for work. I thought I'd try east for a change."

Jackson's squint doesn't lighten up any. Then again, maybe that's how he always looks. He points up to a figure balanced on an eight-inch beam overhead, guiding down a twenty-foot I-beam hung from a derrick cable. Even from this distance I can see that it's the redheaded guy I talked to earlier. "That's Mike O'Reilly. You're going to be working with him bolting those headers." I start climbing up the column next to Mike's, but Jackson grabs me by the arm and pulls me back. By instinct

my hand clenches into a fist, and I unclench it just as quick. I
don't think slugging the boss would be such a good idea. "I'll be
keeping my eye on you," he says, giving me the fish-eye. "If you
can't cut it, your ass will be off the crew by tomorrow."

*Thanks for the pep talk,* I think. I shimmy up the column
with my eyes trained on Mike. He's perched on the beam, wrestling a header into place. I take a few seconds to take in the sight:
his shirt off, his body packed with muscles, his powerful arms
lifted up and struggling with all that steel against the backdrop
of clear blue sky. Pure poetry. Enough to set my dick thumping.
God, I love construction!

Mike is still humping the header when I finally get level with
him, though with twenty feet of empty air still between us.
"Howdy!" I call out to him.

He glances my way and then back at the header. He gives
it a mighty whack with his spud wrench and then looks back
at me again, his gaze bold as brass. His mouth curls up into an
easy smile. "I wondered if you were Pete's replacement. How ya
doing? Did Jackson chew a chunk out of your ass?"

"I still got most of it left." I grab my end of the header. "You
need some help with that?"

"Yeah, if you feel so inclined."

I get the header lined up just so, slip a few bolts in and
tighten the nuts. I glance over to Mike. "You secure?" I call out.
He nods. I hoist myself up onto the beam, trot out to the center
and cut the choker loose. A gust of wind blasts me and I sway
to compensate, nothing to fall back on but empty air. Girder
surfing, we call it back in L.A. The building foundation pit is
a tiny patch of blackness fifty-four stories below. Far enough
down that if I took a dive, parts of me would splatter into
Brooklyn. This doesn't bother me any. If it did, I'd be selling
shoes for a living.

Mike and I pace ourselves like dancers, matching our rhythms and moves as we line up the headers and start bolting them down. I can see Mike knows what he's doing. He works the iron good, moving the beams easily where he wants them and bolting them down quick and skillful. It doesn't take long before we get a heat up good and are snapping those beams into the columns like they're from a kid's erector set.

I find myself sneaking glances at Mike from time to time. He isn't exactly cocky, but he handles himself like a man who knows he's good and just lets his body take over and do what has to be done. It's late in the morning now, and the sun is getting hot. Streams of sweat trickle down his torso, making it fuckin' *gleam*; drops of it bead around his nipples, which are as big as quarters and the color of old pennies. I think about what it'd be like chewing on them, flicking them with my tongue, nipping them with my teeth as Mike's muscular body squirms under me. His torso is nut brown but when he leans down to spin in a low bolt, I see his tan line and a strip of creamy skin beneath it. His ass must be a very pretty thing, pale and smooth like polished ivory. The fun and games a couple of nights ago haven't taken the edge off my hunger; if anything I'm stoked for more of the same.

We're on our fifth header by the time the lunch whistle blows. Mike pulls off his hard hat and wipes his forehead with the back of his hand; I watch as his biceps bulge up and dance. He stands there for a few seconds, his left knee bent, his weight on his right hip, that muscle-packed torso so nicely slicked. I feel my throat squeeze tight just looking at him. He's a slab of prime beef, all right, and my brain goes overtime thinking of all the dirty things I'd like to do to him. He suddenly turns and looks at me, and there's this second when my face is still naked, my thoughts written on it for anyone to see. I couldn't have been more obvious if I'd reached out and grabbed his basket. Mike's eyes burn into me and it's clear he *knows* what's on my mind. But he turns his head and gazes out toward the Jersey shore, like he's searching for something. Slowly, carelessly, he reaches up and scratches his balls, giving them a little extra tug. The signal is so fuckin' blatant that my brain buzzes with confusion. I'm surprised smoke isn't coming out of my ears.

Mike and I eat lunch together sitting on a girder with our legs dangling over eight hundred feet of nothing. Mike is relaxed and friendly, so open and at ease that I begin to wonder if I misread what was going on between us just a few minutes ago. I ask Mike how Pete, the guy whose place I'm taking, happened to fall.

Mike shrugs. "We were working a little late. I guess he was tired and just got sloppy. It happens."

After a while we run out of conversation. I lie on my back and close my eyes, feeling the sun beat down on me. I think about what Mike looks like naked, and I give him a dick that's meaty and thick, just to keep the fantasy interesting. My dick gives a hard thrust against my jeans, but I don't do anything to hide it.

"Thinking about pussy?" Mike asks. I half open my eyes and see him looking down at me, grinning. "I was just wondering. It looks like your dick's about to split your pants open."

"It's been a problem lately," I say, keeping my voice casual. "I seem to be horny all the time."

Mike's grin widens. "Well, maybe you'll get lucky soon." He winks at me, and again I get that weird feeling he's sending me some kind of message. He stands up and dusts himself off. "Time to get back to work."

For the rest of the afternoon it's like that, Mike joking around, giving me these looks that may mean something, but then again maybe not. He's got me wound tighter than a clock, and I don't like it. For one thing, it's affecting my work now. A couple of times I fumble the bolts, stupidly watching them slip between my fingers and drop down all that space beneath us. I almost lose my spud wrench the same way, just grabbing it in the last half second before it's gone for good. I glance toward Mike, and he's watching me, grinning. "Uh-oh," he says. "You almost killed a businessman that time." His smile is good-natured enough, but his eyes gleam with a bold light that misses nothing. He's just having a good ol' time at my expense. I feel like pushing him off his beam.

At 4:45 Jackson signals for us to start wrapping it up. Mike cups his mouth with his hands. "Send another beam up!" he shouts. Jackson shakes his head and points to his watch. "We can do it!" Mike shouts back. "Al and I don't mind working a little late." Jackson shrugs and signals for the crane operator to hoist another beam up.

I glare at Mike. "What the hell's got into you?" I call over to him. "I want to go home."

Mike just grins. "The way you been fucking up this afternoon, I figure you owe the company a few minutes' extra work." The beam swings down overhead, and he guides it into place. Pissed, I help line up the holes and slide a few bolts in. By the time he cuts the choker loose, the rest of the crew has taken off, leaving us alone. I spend a few more minutes bent over my end of the beam, slipping in the remaining bolts and tightening the nuts. I'm working as fast as I can so that I can just get the hell out of here and put an end to this day. I turn to see how Mike's doing with his end. He's still out there on the middle of the beam, only now his pants are down around his ankles. He's slowly stroking his stiff cock, his face as calm as if this is the most natural thing he could be doing. I almost drop my wrench for the second time that day.

"You ought to tie that thing around your wrist," Mike says, "before you kill someone."

I just stare at him. "What the fuck are you doing?"

Mike laughs. "What does it look like?"

I watch him standing there on the beam, beating off. My own dick starts to beat against my zipper, yelling to be let out. "Come on down to where there's some floor beneath us," I say. My throat's so tight I can barely get the words out.

Mike shakes his head. "No. I got a better idea. Come up here and join me."

The beam he's standing on juts out over the side of the building. I look down at the fifty-four stories worth of empty air beneath us. If we fell, I just might be able to shoot a load before hitting bottom, but there'd be hell to pay afterward. I shake my head. "No way, Mike. I only practice safe sex."

But Mike just stands there grinning, stroking his dick. He stops for a minute and peels off his T-shirt. His sweaty torso gleams in the late afternoon sun, cut and chiseled in such a way that every muscle stands out. He tosses the shirt into the wind, and I watch as it floats down into oblivion. The street below is deep in the shadow of early evening, but up here it's still bright day. I spend a couple of seconds watching Mike standing there buck naked except for his hard hat, and I know I'm going to get it on with him or die trying. I jump up on the beam.

"Hold on," Mike calls out. "I want you to get naked first."

*What the hell,* I shrug. I'm ready for anything now. I do a careful strip, draping my clothes over the column head. Seconds later I'm bare-ass naked. A slight breeze plays over my body, and I can feel the last rays of the sun on my skin. The steel's cool and smooth under my bare feet; everything else around me feels like miles of empty air.

Mike's lips curl up into a slow smile. "You look fuckin' great,

Al," he says. He kicks off his shoes, and I watch as they disappear into the darkness below. He steps out of his pants, leaving them piled on the girder behind him.

I walk across the girder toward him like a man crossing pond ice on a sunny day. I've been walking for years on narrow beams above open space, and I feel my body automatically make the tiny adjustments that keep me from losing my balance. When I reach Mike I run my hands over his chest and torso, as much to steady myself as to feel his naked body. He leans forward and kisses me lightly, then not so lightly. We play dueling tongues for a while, and then Mike reaches down and wraps his palm around my dick. He glances at it and then back at me. "Jeez, you got a beautiful dick, Al."

"Yeah, I get a lot of compliments on it."

Mike grins. "I bet. Look how thick it is. And long, too. And how big and red the cockhead is." He laughs. "Not many men have a dick this pretty, Al. I hope you appreciate what you got." He glances down again. "Your balls have a nice size to them, too, even though they're pulled up a little tight."

I give a stiff smile. "Being scared shitless has a way of doing that to me. Maybe we should just skip the commentary and move on to what's next."

Mike looks amused. He carefully bends down and picks up his jeans. He pulls a condom out of the back pocket. "All right, let's get to it. How 'bout plugging my butt hard?"

I have to laugh. "Well, I'm glad you practice safe sex," I say, as I slip the condom on.

I have never fucked with such concentration before. My mind is alert to every movement we make, and my body is as tuned as if each nerve ending has a mind of its own. I begin pumping my hips, first with a slow, grinding tempo, then faster and deeper. Everything is reduced down to one word: balance. Mike knows this too and he meets me stroke for stroke, his body reacting to the thrusts and pulls of mine like we're both well-oiled parts of one moving machine. I hold on to his torso, not roughly, but with a touch light and cautious enough to just barely feel the squirm of his muscles beneath my fingertips. We fuck like we're defusing a bomb, in carefully controlled terror. I have never had sex feel so goddamn exciting.

I spit in my hand and begin stroking Mike off. He groans loudly and squirms against me, a move I wasn't expecting. For a second we sway to one side, and I feel the beam slip from under my feet. Mike and I both quickly shift our weight and regain our balance. "Sweet Jesus," I mutter. But I never miss a stroke.

The lights are beginning to turn on in the buildings below us. The city spreads out beneath us to the horizon, and I feel like I'm fuckin' flying. Even this far up I can still faintly hear the sounds of traffic from below. I plunge deep into Mike again. He cries out and I feel his load gush between my fingers and drip down into the darkness below. I hold on tight as his body shudders in my arms, keeping the control and balance for both of us. When he quiets down, I give my hips a few quick thrusts. That's all I need to get me off. I ride the orgasm out like a surfer on a killer wave, getting off on the thrill but concentrating on my balance all at the same time.

When the last shudder is over, I carefully pull out. Mike turns around and we kiss each other lightly, our bodies pressed tightly together. Mike makes a sudden jerking movement to the side and I feel a half second of pure terror before I regain my balance. He laughs.

I glare at him. "You dickhead."

But Mike just keeps on grinning. He picks up his pants. "Come on; let's get off this damn beam."

Back by the foreman's shack, I give Mike my undershirt to

replace the one he tossed over the side. But he's going to have to take the subway home barefoot. He just shrugs this off. As I get dressed I start thinking about what a fuckin' insane thing it was we just did. To my annoyance, my hands begin to tremble as I tie my shoes. I make sure Mike doesn't see this.

I look up at him. "Did you ever do anything this crazy before?"

The muscles in Mike's face twitch, like he's trying to decide whether or not to say something. Finally he gives a slow, easy smile. "Sure. How do you think the guy you replaced, Pete, fell?" He sees the expression on my face and laughs. "Hey, I was *joking*, okay? I've never done this before."

We ride down in the lift in silence. Mike is idly looking out toward the city skyline. I stare at his face, trying to figure out just exactly how Pete did fall off that girder.

Down on the street, Mike kisses me lightly. "See you tomorrow, Al." I watch as he walks barefoot down the sidewalk to the subway station on the corner, his arms swinging jauntily by his side. I shake my head. Jamming my hands in my jeans pockets, I plow through the crowds of people. When I get to the first street corner, I wait for the light to turn green, looking both ways carefully before crossing.

# DIGGER

Hank Edwards

I notice him right away from my post inside the tiny gas station office; he is difficult to miss. Standing in the middle of the torn-up street, he shovels rocks out of the sand base dumped the day before and smoothes over the rough areas. He works apart from the rest of the crew, bare-chested, with his dirty T-shirt tucked into a back pocket of his faded jeans and a navy blue bandana tied around his head. I let my gaze travel over his body and reach down to shift the swiftly hardening length of my cock to a more comfortable position. He is a big man; around six foot two if he's an inch, with a dark shadow of beard and a deeply tanned and hairy torso. His pecs are big and firm above the slight pouch of a belly that hangs over the droopy, faded waist of his jeans. He stops his work and leans on the handle of his shovel to catch his breath, raising a muscular arm to wipe sweat from his face with the back of his hairy forearm. I take the opportunity to zero in on the dark, hairy tuft of his armpit, and my cock throbs for release.

The gas station where I work sits on the corner of a usually well-traveled intersection. Three months ago, however, two construction projects were started several miles down each of the roads that make up my intersection and now those projects have come together, closing off the roads with battalions of resented orange barrels and routing traffic to other streets. Bulldozers, dirt haulers, some kind of asphalt grinder that tore up the road and threw dust and tar into the air, and a score of sweaty, beefy men all converged on my little corner of the world. I begged the owner to close the doors when the roads were torn up, just shut down for two weeks until the repaving was completed and the drivers could speed even faster down the new asphalt. But the man refused, claiming that the surrounding neighborhood depended on his small shop for milk and other grocery items.

So I sit on the stool and stare out the window at the big man working out in the hot sun. Sweat runs down his face and chest, attracting dirt like a magnet as his tanned skin glistens. I squeeze my fully erect cock once again and have just decided to take a break in the back office and jerk off when the big bear of a man tosses his shovel aside and begins to walk toward the station. I drop my eyes to his wide hips, the denim covering them stained with sweat and dirt, watching breathlessly as he walks closer. His strides are long and strong, the muscles of his legs flexing beneath the faded material of his jeans. His scuffed and dirty work boots kick up clouds of dust as he passes the pumps and crosses the lot. He pulls a dusty T-shirt from his back pocket and wipes off his face then tosses it over his shoulder before pushing through the glass door into the mildly cooler interior of the building.

I sit up straight on my stool, and our eyes lock for a moment when he steps inside. He nods and heads toward the coolers in back, giving me a good look at his sweaty, hairy back, and I groan quietly at the sight. He is the most masculine man I have seen in a long, long time, and my asshole twitches as fantasies explode in my head.

He approaches the glass-enclosed checkout to set three large bottles of water on the counter, then reaches back for his wallet. Sweat stands out on his face and body, and I ache to run my tongue through the thick, dark hair on his chest and lap it up, savoring the salty taste.

"That it?" I ask casually.

"Yeah, it'll do," he responds and looks up at me. "Till you get off work."

I blush, taken aback by his forwardness. "What do you mean?"

"I've seen you watching me," he says in a deep, gravelly voice as he passes money through the metal opening in the glass partition. "Grabbin' your crotch and starin' out the window." He nods to where his shovel lies abandoned in the dirt. "You got me so riled up I had to take a break and come in here to check you out up close." He runs his eyes over my body and grins. "Skinny, but you got hair on your chest so you can't be all bad."

My mouth hangs open and I am at a loss for words as I look down at myself. I weigh in at 190 pounds with blond hair, blue eyes, and dark blond hair on my chest and back. I shift my weight and look back up at him, completely at a loss for words.

He smiles. "Come to my place when you get off work." Turning to look around, he says, "Unless you're the only one here."

I shrug and glance nervously out the window, noticing that the rest of his crew has departed for lunch and we are, indeed, alone. "Well, yeah, I am. But—"

He tips his head back. "Let me in there."

"I can't do that."

"Okay, then meet me out here," he says and smiles. "My crew will be back in half an hour so we don't have much time."

My stomach is in knots as I take the key and step out the reinforced door to his side of the glass. Once I get through the door I can smell his sweat, and my stomach knots harder as my cock strains at my jock, eager to be free and in the grip of this big, sweaty bear of a man. He turns to face me, the navy blue bandana tied around his head catching the steel of his eyes.

"Let's go back here," he says and reaches out to grab me by the front of my shorts and pull me to the rear of the store where he stops and turns to face me. "You like sweat?"

I lick my dry lips and nod, my eyes locked on his face. He pulls me into him, crushing me against his sweaty body as his lips mash mine, his tongue filling my mouth. A grunt rumbles in my throat at the heat of his kiss, and I raise my hands to palm his sweaty, dirty chest. My fingers find his nipples and pinch.

"Harder," he growls into my mouth as his whiskers rake my clean-shaven jaw. "Pull on 'em."

I tighten my grip on his tits and pull on the hardening nipples, but they are slippery with sweat and my fingers have trouble keeping hold. He becomes impatient and pulls his mouth off mine to press my face down into the hairy, sweaty slickness of his chest. "Bite 'em."

My teeth nip and tug at his nipples as my hands move over his body. I run my left hand over the sweaty, hairy expanse of his back as my right one runs down over the slick surface of his belly to squeeze the bulge in his jeans. His cock is hard and long, extending down the length of his right thigh, and I groan at the feel of its heat through the denim.

"Oh, that's nice," he moans. "Squeeze that cock. Yeah, that's it."

His big, hairy hand moves down my back and slips beneath my shorts where he cups my hairy left cheek. He moves his hand to my asscrack and slides a sweaty finger down its length to the wet heat of my clenched asshole where he rubs in a slow, circular motion.

"Loosen 'er up, buddy," he says in a low voice. "Let my finger in there. That's it, ease it open."

His blunt, thick finger slips deep into my anus, and I sigh and groan against the wet heat of his chest. As I move my head to the side he raises his arm to allow me to bury my face in his sweat-soaked armpit. He smells rank and masculine, and I breathe it in deep before opening my mouth and running my tongue through the thick hair of his pit. I snuffle and snort all along his hairy hollow, slurping up his sweat as he pokes his finger deep into my ass. I rub my face all around the fragrant bush of his armpit and then move back to his chest to suck his nipples once again.

Firm pressure on the back of my head moves me lower along his body until my face is pressed against the dirty, sweaty crotch of his jeans. I grab the denim-covered length of his cock in my teeth and bite up and down along the shaft. He must be seven inches long, at least, and thick.

"You've got a hot hole," he says as his finger prods deeper still. He bends it slightly and twists it inside me.

"Oh, fuck," I gasp. "Get that hole." I fumble with his zipper until his jeans fall open and slide down his legs, revealing big, hairy thighs that bookend a thick, uncut cock and a set of hairy, sweaty, low-hung balls. My asshole tightens around his finger at the sight of his dick and he chuckles.

"You like that meat, huh?" he says. "Want that big bear cock up your tight ass?"

"Oh, yeah," I reply then grab his dick and stroke it a few times before opening my mouth to take as much as I can handle down my throat. The smell of his sweat fills my head as my nose dips into his damp, dirty bush. His cock is a hot, thick, salty slab of meat lying along my tongue, and I slowly ease it out of my mouth to pull the foreskin back, exposing the wide, peach-colored head on which I plant a deep, sucking kiss.

"Yeah, that's the way," he sighs and burrows a second finger up beside his first, both drilling my asshole faster and faster as I suck on the head of his cock. "Get that head. Suck it good and hard."

I release my grip on his dick and suck him all-out, moving my mouth more quickly up and down along his hard pole as I grab his sweat-sticky nuts and pull them taut. He grunts and reaches down to hold my head still as his hips come to life and he fucks my face. The long, thick length of him jabs deep into my throat, choking me with every thrust, and I squeeze my eyes closed to focus on relaxing my throat. He has two fingers up my ass and his cock pumping into my gullet as I pull on his balls and brace myself against the hard muscle of his thigh.

"Man, I just gotta get a taste of your cock," he says and slips his fingers out of my hole as he pulls his dick from between my lips. I watch his cock pull away, gleaming with my spit, then he pulls me upright and pushes my shorts and jock down before lifting me up to the counter in the back corner of the store next to the fountain-pop dispenser. My circumcised dick stands straight up along my belly, precum flowing down the seven-inch shaft like sexual lava. He bends over and swallows me in one gulp, pressing his whiskered face into my lap as his tongue rolls around my cock.

"Uh!" I grunt, closing my eyes and resting my head back against the wall. He sucks me hard and deep, pulling on his own cock as he works mine over with his mouth. I pull off my tank top, and he slides his free hand up to pinch a nipple then cups my armpit, sliding his fingers through the sweaty hair.

Easing my legs over his strong, hairy shoulders, he lets my cock flop out of his mouth as he moves down to suck my balls. His tongue, wide and hot, slathers over my hairy sac as he jacks his cock and moves his other hand down from my armpit to begin stroking my dick. He sucks my nuts into his mouth and closes his lips over them tight, pulling back then shaking his head slowly from side to side.

"Oh, suck my balls, yeah," I groan and reach down to put my hands on the navy bandana still tied around his head. It comes off in my fingers and I find he is bald, a short cropped ring of hair traveling from ear to ear, and I moan deeper as I bring his sweat-soaked bandana to my face and breathe in his scent. I have always been drawn to big, burly, bald men; this guy is a dream come true.

His tongue pushes my balls from between his lips, and the spit-slick sac lolls over his nose as he digs into my hot, sweaty hole, burying his mouth in my ass. The scrape of his whiskers against my sensitive sphincter makes me wild, and I plant my hands on the back of his head to press his face harder against me. His tongue flicks out to stroke the pink pucker of my anus, slicking it with spit that he pushes deeper inside with a thick finger.

He stands up suddenly, his log of a cock slapping against the counter and brushing along my thigh as he slides two fingers deep into my ass and turns his head to inspect the display racks. Leaning over, he grabs a box of condoms with his free hand and holds it up.

"Pay for these later, will ya?" he asks with a grin.

"Yeah," I gasp and pout a little when he retracts his fingers from my tingling and twitching hole to tear open the box and a packet from inside. My gut clenches as he lets a thick, white glob of spit fall onto the head of his dick before he rolls the condom along the veined and throbbing shaft.

He steps up between my legs, positions himself at the threshold of my body then penetrates me with a slow, steady thrust. My mouth falls open and my head tips back as he pushes himself into me. My rectal muscles clench then release, opening up before his invading prick and closing back around it in a slick, wet embrace.

"Oh, fuck," he moans, his eyes closed and sweat running down his face. "You've got a tight fuckhole."

"Stretch that fuckin' ass out," I reply and lean forward to kiss him, my tongue bursting past his lips and tangling with his own. "Fuck me."

He stands still for a moment as we kiss, his cock fully embedded inside my ass, then he pulls his hips back and rams himself deeper into me. I grunt as his thrust almost knocks the wind out of me and my eyes pop open wide. I clench the muscles all along my anal tract as he pulls out, gripping him tight, and he groans before driving it back home again.

I reach back and grab a fistful of his hairy, sweaty asscheeks in both hands as he pounds his cock up my ass. He stuffs his thick, uncut dick into my tight, battered hole faster, his strokes becoming deeper and more forceful. He kisses me again, his tongue hot and tasting of my sweaty ass as I listen to the pop and squelch of his cock punching in and pulling out of my asshole as well as the wet, solid spank of his sweaty, dirty skin meeting mine.

"Oh, fuck, you're fuckin' hole is fuckin' tight," he manages before his expression contorts. He sucks in his breath and screws up his face, leaning back and reaching up to grab my ankles where they bounce in the air. "Oh, fuck! I'm gonna shoot. Oh, yeah, I'm fuckin' comin'!"

I take hold of my painfully hard cock and stroke it furiously. His thrusts become slower, deeper as he pumps his load into the tip of the condom buried high up inside my hole. I use my muscles to bite down on his cock, keeping him inside me as I jerk myself to orgasm.

"Oh, yeah," I alert him and then hear the wet pop as my load erupts all over my hairy chest and belly. He watches the cum splatter across my torso and moans encouragement, shallowly pumping into me with his slowly softening dick as sweat drips off his nose. Reaching down, he spreads the thick, sticky semen across my sweaty skin then rubs it into each of my nipples before raising his eyes to look in my face.

"That was fuckin' hot," he says.

"Yeah," is all I can think to say back.

"What's your name?" he asks with a smile.

"David. What's yours?"

"Bill."

"Nice to meet you, Bill," I say and we laugh.

He eases himself out of me, and I watch as he carefully pulls the condom off his dick, the thick, white cum in the tip sloshing around as he looks for a trash can.

"I'll take care of it," I say, and he hands it over with a sexy grin.

"I bet you will." He pulls up his jeans, adjusts his thick, sweaty package and ties the bandana around his head with practiced ease. "Thanks for lunch," he says with a wink. "What time do you get off?"

"Five," I reply as I search for my jockstrap. He had pulled it off and tossed it somewhere but now I cannot find it.

"I'll come by at five, unshowered, to give this back to you." I turn to find him holding my damp, sweaty jockstrap up to his face, breathing in the musky odor of my crotch. My cock twitches at the sight, a motion he notices with a cocked eyebrow.

"We'll head back to my apartment," he says as I quickly pull on my shorts and walk him to the door. He grabs his bottles of water and heads outside to shamble back across the lot to his shovel, my jockstrap stuffed in his front pocket. I pay for the box of condoms and try to find a comfortable spot on my stool, but my asshole will have none of it. It's hungry for more cock, and I cannot sit still. I tie a knot in the open end of the condom, trapping his cum inside, then slip it in the front pocket of my shorts. I'll decide later what I'm going to do with it.

I pace behind the counter, fingering the condom and watching as he works in the heat and dust. Every so often Bill looks up and smiles at me through the glass, reaching back to take my jockstrap from his pocket and use it to wipe his face. When I'm not watching Bill, I watch the clock and think that an afternoon has never lasted this long.

# WORKING THE WEEKEND

Neil Plakcy

B ut it's Thanksgiving weekend," I said to my boss. "I'll never be able to convince a crew to work through the holiday."

"You want to be a construction manager, you figure out a way to get a crew in there," he said.

"Can I offer them a cash bonus?"

He shook his head. "Look, Danny, we're over budget and behind schedule. If you don't get those sprinkler mains installed by Monday morning, we won't be able to hang the ceilings, and that's going to fuck our whole schedule." He looked up from the drawings in front of him. "And if the schedule gets fucked, we're going to have to start lying off guys to save money."

He didn't have to say it outright. I was the most junior construction manager, the last hired and the first to be fired. Especially if I couldn't do a simple thing like convince the sprinkler contractor to work through the weekend laying pipe through the west wing of the mall we were building.

I walked out of the trailer and onto the site. I tracked down Vinny, the superintendent for the sprinkler contractors, at the roach coach getting a cup of coffee. "Hey, just the man I wanted to see," I said, coming up to him.

Vinny was the kind of guy they coined the phrase "Italian Stallion" for. Just under six feet tall, he had a swarthy complexion and a head of thick black hair. He was in his early thirties, handsome and muscular. A thick gold chain peeked through his open shirt collar, nestled in chest hair: sex on wheels.

I explained the problem. "No fucking way," he said. "Danny boy, it's Wednesday afternoon. My guys are all set to take off for the holiday. Even if I wanted to, I couldn't get a crew together to work the weekend."

I begged, I pleaded, I threatened. No dice. Finally, Vinny stalked away. "Man, what did you do to get Vinny's panties in such a twist?"

I looked over and saw one of Vinny's crew, a young guy named Jeff. He was about my age, early twenties, slim-hipped and wiry. He'd been working late one night a week or before, and I'd found him alone in one of the bays at the far end of the mall. One thing had led to another, ending with me bent over a pile of pipe and Jeff driving his dick up my ass.

I'd thought it was a one-time thing. I heard the guys teasing Jeff about his girlfriend and how she didn't like to put out, and I figured I was just a temporary stopgap. That was fine with me. There was a construction site full of good-looking guys (and some that weren't so good looking but still had big dicks), and I enjoyed providing the occasional service when they were hard up—or just hard.

I explained to Jeff about the need to get a crew together to work over the weekend. "Paying overtime?" he asked.

I shrugged. "That's up to Vinny, but he's got a penalty clause in his contract if he doesn't finish on time. Overtime would be a lot cheaper than the penalty."

"Let me talk to him," he said.

An hour passed. I was back in my office in the trailer, wondering what kind of job I could get if I were fired, when Vinny walked in. "Here's your shopping list," he said. "Have all this stuff and be here at seven on Friday morning."

He dropped the paper on my desk and walked out.

The first item was *Condoms. Assorted. Some ribbed, some extralarge.*

What the fuck?

The second item was lube. The word *plenty* was underlined next to it.

Friday morning, I showed up on-site at seven, as directed. The parking lot was empty except for a truck with the sprinkler company's logo on the side. Two pickups pulled in right behind me.

Jeff was in one pickup and Vinny in the truck. The second pickup belonged to Cal, a skinny blond guy to whom I had never spoken. "We take our first break at ten," Vinny said, pulling pipe out of the back of the van. "Be ready."

What the fuck did that mean? I had the bag full of condoms and lube. What else was I supposed to do?

I worked in the trailer for a couple of hours, finishing paper-work, and around nine forty-five, I walked out to the west wing. I heard a radio blasting '60s oldies, and the sound of hammers on metal. Just before ten, Vinny came climbing down from the ceiling. He was wearing a white hard hat with the contractor's logo on it, a T-shirt, jeans and sneakers. "You're not ready," he said.

"What do you mean? I've got the stuff."

"Get naked."

I looked around. "Here?"

He peeled off his T-shirt. "Hell, yeah. You got a better place?"

It wasn't exactly the most romantic proposition I'd ever gotten, but it'd do. I stripped down, dropping my T-shirt and jeans over a sawhorse. When I turned back to him, I saw his sausage, already half-hard, and shivered. It wasn't that long, but damn, it was thick. He was naked except for his white socks and his matching white hard hat.

Out of the corner of my eye, I saw Jeff and Cal heading toward a big thermos of coffee. Both of them were dressed as Vinny'd been, jeans and T-shirts, though they both wore blue hard hats.

"Get me ready," Vinny said to me.

"Vinny. I know what to do," I said.

"Yeah, that's what Jeff said."

I pulled a big piece of carpet insulation over and laid it in front of him then dropped to my knees. I licked up and down the length of his dick and felt him shiver. Then I took him inside me, bobbing up and down as if I was going for apples at a Halloween party. I licked and sucked, tonguing his balls, until finally he pulled my head back.

"I need the extralarge," Vinny said. "Suit me up."

I ripped open a condom, unfurled it and slid it over his stiff prick. Vinny had a decent body for a guy in his midthirties: thick, hairy calves and thighs; the start of a potbelly and big fat pecs with tight brown nipples. His dick stood out from a thatch of thick, wiry black hair. He still wore his gold necklace, his gold watch and his wedding ring.

Then I turned and bent over the sawhorse, folding my jeans under my abdomen. My bare feet rested on the unfinished concrete, and I steadied myself by grabbing the edges of a big metal tool chest. I felt the cool air on my exposed butthole, the pressure of the wood and cloth on my own hard dick.

Out of the corner of my eye, I saw Jeff and Cal had their jeans open, stroking their dicks. "Cal!" Vinny barked. "Lose the pants and get over here."

Cal did as he was ordered. The skinny guy was still wearing his T-shirt, hard hat and white socks. His pelvis was as flat as a board, and his half-hard dick swung between his legs as he walked. "Get him lubed up for me," Vinny said.

"Yes, boss," Cal said. He squirted some lube in his hand, coating his palm and fingers. Then he started smearing it around my asshole. The lube was cold and gave my butt goose bumps, but when he started fingering my hole, I warmed up fast.

"All right, Jeff, get your ass over here and get me lubed up," Vinny said.

I looked over at Jeff. Slowly, tantalizingly, he peeled his T-shirt off. He had rock-hard abs and bulging biceps. He kicked off his shoes, then started shimmying his jeans down over his hips.

"This ain't no striptease, boy," Vinny said. "Get moving."

"Fuck you," Jeff said, with a smile. He kept on shimmying.

The feeling of Cal's hand on my ass and his finger up my chute was sending tremors through me, and I wanted Vinny's fat sausage up there fast. "Come on, Jeff," I panted. "You heard the boss."

Jeff laughed. He dropped his jeans and walked over, still wearing his white briefs, his white tube socks and his blue hard hat. He took a handful of lube and started smearing it on Vinny's dick, while he leaned down and took Vinny's left nipple between his teeth.

"Dammit, Jeff, you know what that does to me," Vinny said, short of breath.

"Yeah," Jeff said, taking a moment's break. "I do."

Cal got two fingers into my ass. They were rough and

calloused, and he got them both in up to the second joint, but they were only fingers. I wanted something more. "Hello," I said. "Waiting for a dick here."

Vinny pushed Jeff and Cal aside, grabbed my hips and aimed his dick at my hole. There was a moment's pain as he slammed into me, but then I discovered Cal had worked his way under the sawhorse and taken my stiff dick in his mouth. I was in heaven, being plowed on one end and sucked on the other.

Vinny was right; he'd needed the extralarge condom. It felt like he was splitting my ass in two, as if somebody had rammed a baseball bat up there. Nevertheless, I was well lubed, thanks to Cal, and his mouth on my dick was taking my mind off the pain in my ass.

Behind me, I heard the tear of a condom wrapper and the squirt of more lube, and then Vinny slammed into me extrahard. The pain was like an electric shock running through my body. "Dammit, Jeff," I heard Vinny say.

"Come on, boss, take it like a man," Jeff said.

I looked down. Cal was on his back, his hard hat lying next to him, as he sucked my dick. Behind me, Jeff was fucking the shit out of Vinny, and every time he slammed into Vinny, Vinny slammed into me.

I started panting and whimpering, and I couldn't hold back any longer. I shot off in Cal's mouth, and then a moment later I felt Vinny shoot up my ass. Jeff howled, and I figured that meant he'd gotten off, too.

We pulled apart. Vinny looked at his watch. "We break for lunch at twelve," he said. "This time, you'd better be ready, Danny, if you expect us to finish. Hell, this job could take us all weekend."

"I'll do anything I can to keep the work going," I said.

I pulled on my T-shirt and jeans and limped back to the

trailer. I couldn't sit down for a half hour; Vinny had really done a number on my ass. And I had to be back on duty at noon. Around eleven-thirty I ran out to the local sub shop and bought everybody sandwiches and sodas. Back at the site, I laid a wooden door over a pair of sawhorses, stripped down and set everything out. I brought three folding chairs out from the trailer. Then I climbed up on the makeshift table and made myself the centerpiece.

"Damn! Laid out on a platter," Vinny said when he climbed down from the ceiling. "Isn't that a pretty sight?"

The other guys followed him down. They each took a sandwich and a soda and sat down around the table. I propped myself up on one elbow while they ate around me. Occasionally one of them would feed me a potato chip or reach over to tweak a nipple.

Vinny finished his sandwich, crumpled up the wrapping paper and said, "Now for dessert." He stood up and started to unbuckle his jeans. I scooted up to the end of the table so I could take his fat sausage in my mouth. I nearly gagged when he first slammed it into me, so I backed off a little and started licking and sucking the big, circumcised knob.

"Yeah, suck that dick, Danny. Suck it like a porn star."

As I kept on sucking, I felt Cal's tongue at my asshole, licking and eating at me. My body started quivering like the indicator on a level as I took Vinny deeper and deeper, feeling his pubic hair tickling my nose.

When I looked up, I could see Jeff behind Cal, fucking his ass. After a couple of minutes, Vinny pulled his dick out of my mouth and said, "Roll over on your back, Danny."

I did as instructed. "Jeff, you get up there," Vinny said, and Jeff climbed up on the makeshift table, kicking away the debris of lunch. He was naked except for his white socks and blue hard hat, and he squatted over me, presenting me with his ass.

I grabbed hold of it and started eating for all I was worth. I licked my way around his hole, then folded my tongue up and started poking away at him. From the shivers he was giving off, I figured he liked it.

Behind me, I could see Cal on his knees sucking the boss, who was watching Jeff and me eagerly, rubbing his thumbs around his stiff brown nipples that were nestled in a forest of thick black chest hair. They stood up like tiny dicks. Then Jeff stood up and walked down the table a few feet. He squatted, grabbed a handful of lube, greased my dick and then positioned himself over me.

He sat down on me tentatively at first, then leveraging his strong thighs and calves up and down, clenched his ass muscles around my pole. His own dick bounced up and down in front of me tantalizingly while I did my best to fuck his ass from that position, moving my hips up as he came down, and sweat began to drip off his chest and onto mine. Eventually he grabbed himself with one hand and started jerking, and just as I began erupting up his ass, he shot off across my chest.

He pulled off me and jumped off the makeshift table, my come dripping out of his ass. He reached down below, wagged his finger around up there and then wiped it against my thigh.

Vinny pulled his dick out of Cal's mouth just as he was ready to shoot, and his come joined Jeff's on my chest. "Better get this mess cleaned up," Vinny said. "We'll be taking another break at three thirty."

"Damn," I said. "How long are you guys gonna work?"

"Till we get 'er done," he said. "You're the turkey that hired us this weekend, and you're gonna get pretty damned stuffed by the time we're done."

"Yes, boss," I said. They pulled their clothes and hard hats back on and climbed back up the ladder to the ceiling, and I struggled up from the table. My dick had been drained and my ass rammed, and it was only the start of a long weekend.

At our Monday morning construction meeting, my boss complimented me on getting all the sprinkler mains installed. "Hell of an initiative, getting that all accomplished," he said. "How'd you convince them?"

"Turkey," I said. "And stuffing. Lots of it."

# FROZEN STIFF

H. L. Champa

I had never been so cold in my entire life. There was nothing in any book I'd read about how the wind bit at your skin, causing pain I never knew existed. Nothing in the literature they had sent me before I arrived in Antarctica prepared me for the reality of it. I had ventured out into the frigid air only a few times since my arrival three months before, and it always shocked my system. I was wearing six layers of clothing and still felt the icy chill in my bones. Getting dressed to brave the elements had become a more arduous chore than slogging through huge columns of data. Under all that material, I couldn't do anything but stand there, watching the others do work. Observing was really my only job anyway. As a pencil pusher, I didn't need to be there when they dug the ice cores. However, I had ulterior motives substantial enough to make me brave the cold. His name was Frank, head driller and director of maintenance, and the hottest guy a nerd like me had ever seen.

My fingers barely moved in my giant gloves. Despite the fur

and down lining of my bright orange parka, the damn wind still got in. Standing on one of the biggest glaciers in the world, watching the giant machine piercing the ice, I again cursed myself for agreeing to make the trek out to the ice field. I had never let my dick think for me before, and it had sure picked a lousy time to pipe up. I could have ogled Frank anywhere on base, indoors with the heat blasting. But for some reason, when he asked me if I wanted to watch the ice-drilling, I said yes. My brain didn't have time to stop me. Now my whole body was shouting at me, telling me what an idiot I was. Frank and I had had a few conversations, and I had been searching for a way to get closer to him. Since we had little else in common but the ice, I felt like I had no choice. I just hoped I didn't freeze to death before I had the chance to kiss him.

The huge drill sent noise out for miles, with nothing in sight to stop or block it. Shuffling my spike-bottomed boots on the rough ice, I fought to stay upright as the gales blasted across the open expanse of pure white. The drill came to a shaking halt, and the ice core was gently winched up to the surface of the glacier. As we maneuvered the ice for transport, Frank shoved past me to secure the precious cargo. Between the wind and his strong push, I was flat on the ice before I knew it. Staring up into the bluest sky I'd ever seen, I realized I couldn't move. Like a turtle on its shell, I didn't quite know how to right myself. As I began to struggle, a large shadow fell over my face.

"Sorry, Harvard. My fault. I forgot you were tagging along today. Let me help you."

Frank grabbed my parka and yanked me back to my feet with surprisingly little effort. Standing in front of him, I felt as small as I had on my first day of junior high school. He was a regular at the station, doing nine-month stints for the last five years. Without guys like him, we science geeks would have died on the ice years ago. Our studies got all the attention, but he did the real work. My tumble reminded me again of how helpless Antarctica made me feel.

"You okay?"

"Yeah, I'm fine. Just a bump, no big deal."

"The ice is slippery, you know. Think a smart guy like you would have picked up on that by now."

My searing embarrassment ebbed a little when Frank winked and slapped my shoulder before going back to the drill. He walked on the ice as if he had done it all his life, and his giant parka didn't slow him down one bit. He called me "kid," even though he was barely a year older than I was. He only ever referred to people by monikers and handles. He said it was easier than learning a completely new list of names every few months. We were all just temporary, flowing in and out like tide. He was as close to permanent as anything got in Antarctica. Everyone loved Frank. His stories were the stuff of legend, as he had seen and done it all. Literally. I had heard more about Frank's many conquests than warnings about the cold. It got lonely at the South Pole, after all. But from what I had heard through the relentless grapevine, Frank was taking a break from his normal routine. Just my luck. I jumped on the truck with the ice, having seen enough drilling for one day. Frank shot me a mocking salute as we sped away, the drill kicking back to life again, the sound filling the profound silence.

My fall wasn't the first time I had humiliated myself in front of Frank. There had been a million little incidents over the last few months. But the capper came when I had to make a trip to the infirmary to get my head stitched up. I had dropped my pen in the lab and after bending to retrieve it from beneath the table where it had rolled, I cracked my head on the metal underside. As I sat on the paper-covered table waiting for the doctor to thread the needle, Frank came in. He had dislocated a finger on a drilling trip and while I stared in awe, the other doctor yanked on the finger till, with a crack, it slipped back to its rightful place. I felt my stomach lurch and the next thing I remember was waking up with Frank and two doctors staring at me. I had fainted.

"Wow, that was amazing, kid. You dropped right over. Classic."

I was still trying to live that one down.

Back at base, I was finally able to shed all my layers and move around again. In the lab, I could forget my fall and my poorly thought out plan to get close to Frank. In the lab, I was competent and in control. Outside, well, that was a different story. After a few hours of data collection, I needed a break. Heading to the mess hall, I passed Frank, fresh from the freezing cold and still red in the face. He stopped when he saw me, clapping a huge hand down on my shoulder.

"Hey, college. How's the number-crunching going?"

"Fine. You know, there's still a lot of data to get through. But, we are finding some pretty interesting carbon dioxide levels in the turn-of-the-century core segments."

"Sounds riveting. You and I must have different definitions of what is interesting. I was just going to watch the replay of the game with the guys. You wanna come?"

Having no idea which game or even what type of game he was talking about, I smiled politely and shook my head.

"I don't think so, Frank. I've got a million things to do after dinner, and I'm not much of a sports guy. But thanks anyway."

"You know, you shouldn't take life so seriously, kid. Everyone needs a distraction. Otherwise this place can drive you crazy."

"I've heard that. Got any suggestions?"

"I could think of one or two things that could keep you busy."

I watched with a gulp as Frank raised his left eyebrow suggestively. His hand lingered on my shoulder, his fingers digging into my skin harder than I was used to. I wanted to pull away, but something held my feet to the floor. His eyes cut right through me, the wide smile on his face impossible to look away from.

"See you later, kid."

I watched him walk away, my heart flipping over more than a few times. For a split second, I was tempted to follow him and give having fun a chance. Instead, I chose the easy path and followed the smell of soup to the mess hall. I didn't have the heart to tell him I was already distracted.

I got to the lab after dinner, ready to tackle a new set of ice-core data and finally finish getting caught up on the sediment collection research. Instead, I found all the computers down and none of the instruments working. I picked up the phone to call for help, but it was dead too. Pushing open the lab door, I headed to the maintenance office in the hopes of finding Frank, but when I got to the office, he was nowhere to be found. Remembering the aforementioned game, I headed to the television room, expecting to find a rowdy and loud group of guys shouting instructions to the team on the screen. Instead, I found an empty room except for Frank, who was fiddling with the wires behind the set. The snow on the screen was as harsh as any outside. Cursing, Frank stood up and noticed me standing in the doorway.

"Hey, kid. What's up? If you're here for the game, forget it. The satellite is down. We're not getting anything right now."

"I guess that explains why the computers in the lab are down."

"Yeah, we lost our connection. It should be up by morning."

I sighed, the thoughts of another hellish day of work filling my head. Frank chuckled as he watched me fret. He grabbed a beer that was perched on the television and took a long drink.

"What were you doing in the lab at this hour? Didn't I tell you, you need to have some fun?"

"You may have mentioned it. I told you, I just have a ton of work to do."

"Do you ever do anything besides work? I mean, I never see you at any of the movies or events. You know, you are allowed to enjoy yourself every once in a while. I'm sure the eggheads back home won't mind."

"I don't think I know how."

He plunked down on the couch, and I decided to join him. I had never been alone with Frank before as the station was always buzzing with activity and people. It was a small group, but it was an even smaller base.

"So, what do we do now, since there's no game to watch?"

"I was going to go out and check the generators. You wanna come?"

"That's your idea of fun? And you had the nerve to tease me."

"Come on, it won't be so bad. Besides, it's a pretty amazing view."

"Of what?"

"Tell me you haven't been outside at night yet?"

"Are you crazy? It's cold enough during the day."

Frank stood up, grabbing my barely touched beer and setting it down on the table in front of us.

"Go get dressed and meet me back here. There's something you need to see."

* * *

I trudged down the metal hallway, my crampons scraping against the floor. I waddled back to the television room and found Frank standing in the hall, waiting. He didn't say a word when he saw me, just motioned for me to follow him to the door to the outside. As he pushed it open, I felt that familiar sting in my eyes; the bitter bite of the freezing air hit me. He grabbed my hand and pulled me along the building, leading me in the opposite direction from the generators. I blinked to focus my eyes, but I could barely see in front of me. We turned to the left, and he stopped abruptly. So had the wind. I was stunned, since the roar of it was still all around us, but for some reason we were safe. I pulled my hood back, looking around to find us tucked between the base buildings and the garage where the equipment was stored. Everything was black, the few lights from the base blocked out by the garage. I could just make out Frank's silhouette. The silence seemed deeper in the dark, the quiet almost eerie.

"I think we missed the generators."

"They can wait. I told you there's something you've got to see."

"What?"

"Look up."

Tilting my head back, I finally saw them. There were a million stars above us, piercing the black sky like little flashlights. It had never occurred to me to look, never occurred to me to venture out at night. I was always too scared. Each way I looked there were new constellations to see, filling every possible space in the sky. It was amazing. I looked at Frank, who, instead of looking up, was looking right at me.

"Pretty amazing, aren't they, kid?"

"Yeah. I can't believe I never did this before."

"I told you. Sometimes you just have to take a break. And take a look at what is right in front of you."

"This is great, Frank. Thanks for bringing me out here."

We stood in the most beautiful silence, the sky offering up its boundless possibilities. I knew I should say something, do something. This might be my only chance, alone in the dark with Frank. I turned and took two steps toward him, but I felt my feet start to give way beneath me. I was thankful when I felt Frank grab on to my parka and pull me to him. He leaned down, his face right in front of mine. I could barely make out his eyes, the dark was so thick all around us. My body weight was resting against him, my toes still stuck into the ice.

"Thanks, Frank. Wow, twice in one day. You're my hero."

"Goes with the job. I told you to be careful."

I expected him to let me go, just as he had earlier in the day. Instead, his hands moved around my back, crushing me as close to him as our coats would allow. His nose bumped mine, the cold tip rubbing over my cheek.

"Frank, what are you doing?"

"Something we should have done a long time ago. I've been patient with you, kid, but I'm tired of waiting. Besides, I don't want to take the chance of you falling through the ice and disappearing."

His smile faded, and his lips brushed against mine, the hot breath from his mouth a welcome respite from the cold. I reached up for his neck, my thick, gloved fingers just managing to hold on as he claimed my mouth. I let his tongue in, pressing back with my own, our heat mingling in the frigid air. Easing away, he left me gasping, the cold air again assaulting my lungs. I was too stunned to speak, words failing me for the first time in my life.

Frank didn't speak either, just led me back inside, down the twisted series of corridors, right to the door of his room.

I was sweating by the time we arrived, all my layers trapping every ounce of heat my body was throwing off. He shoved his door open, pushing me inside before letting the metal slam shut. He started yanking at my parka, pulling the thick plastic-coated zipper down and shoving the orange fabric to the floor. Discarding his own, he was back in front of me, his huge body towering over me. He tugged me forward by the suspenders attached to my snow pants, our faces once again inches apart. His tongue reached out and touched my bottom lip, and I pulled back instinctively.

"Frank, I don't think…"

"That's your problem, Andrew. You're always thinking too much."

He looked at me, his crooked smile making me sweat a little bit more. His hands remained wrapped tight around the elastic suspenders, only letting me get so far away before he jerked me back toward him. His response to my stunned look brought me back down to earth.

"What? You thought I didn't know your name?"

"I'm just surprised, is all. I don't think I've ever heard you say it. Ever."

"You'd be amazed what I can remember about researchers with really cute asses."

He hauled me closer until I felt his big chest pressed against mine. I tried not to flinch when he grabbed a handful of my hair, tilting my face toward his. His thick fingers forced a gasp from my mouth, despite my efforts to keep it in. He took full advantage of my open mouth, overwhelming me with his lips and tongue. I felt like I couldn't breathe, and my body went limp against Frank's sturdy frame. He slid my suspenders and thick snow pants to the floor, each layer revealing another that needed to be discarded. We broke our kiss, our mouths restless as we peeled back each layer of material hoping to find the last. Finally, his hands were at the hem of my white T-shirt. It was the first layer I had put on that morning. As he pulled the cotton over my head, I tried not to feel self-conscious about my lack of muscles. We stood amongst our piles of clothing, each of us down to our boxer shorts. Compared to Frank, I felt like a teenager again. His chest was broad, with dark hair covering almost every inch. I couldn't resist touching him, and my palms ran down his hot skin until I got to his hard abs. He stopped me, grabbing my wrists before I got any farther. It hurt, but I liked it. His eyes bored into me, just like the drill he used all the time. I swallowed, my cock stirring in anticipation.

"Get on the bed, on your knees."

I hesitate for a second, frozen to the spot where I stood. My logical brain was trying to formulate a way for me to object, but the rest of my body was overriding my reasonable side. Apparently, Frank thought I was taking too long, and with a quick shove, he sent me tumbling onto his mattress, my knees pressing into the springs. Before I could move, he grabbed my boxers and forced them down, leaving my ass naked in front of him. His hands smoothed over my cheeks, my cock bobbing free, waiting for attention. I winced at the thick press of his fingers on my skin, the rough way he pulled my cheeks apart. I had never felt more exposed, more at the mercy of someone else's whims. My forehead rested on my hands as I waited for Frank to do something. Long seconds stretched out, and the only sound in the room was our breathing. Finally, I felt a finger drag over my puckered hole in a quick tease, over as soon as it started. His finger returned, this time moistened with saliva. He circled my opening before pressing the tip gently inside me, his other hand closing around my cock. His fist moved up and down on my stiff dick, my moans escaping my throat for the first time.

"You want me to lick that sweet little asshole?"

I desperately wanted to answer him, but my voice was not working. I tried to nod, but I just heard Frank laughing behind me. His finger stopped moving, his hand disappearing from my cock. I whimpered in distress, turning to look at his impassive face.

"That's not good enough, kid. I need to hear it. Come on, you know you want it. Just tell me. I wanna hear the words come out of that uptight little mouth of yours."

"Frank, please. I can't."

"Sure you can. Tell me, or I'll find something else to keep me busy tonight."

I sighed, my body screaming out in protest, unable to bear any more. I pushed my ass back toward Frank, my desiccated mouth forming the words my head was already shouting.

"Lick my asshole, Frank. Please, I want to feel your tongue on me."

I didn't have to wait long for Frank to oblige me. His tongue dove right in, nothing teasing or gentle about it. The tip went right for my center, pushing my asshole open little by little. His fist returned to my cock, which was aching to be touched. I couldn't stop myself from rocking back into him, trying to get more of his fat tongue in me, but he stayed firmly in control, his tongue easing away, going back to featherlight licks around my rim. His hand stroked my cock at an erratic pace, keeping me guessing and frustrated. I groaned at the torture, but I loved every second of it. Frank was groaning too, pushing his tongue back into my ass, wiggling and squirming his way deeper inside me. I was so close to coming, my whole body was beginning to shake with the strain. Frank replaced his tongue with his finger, his thick digit slipping inside to the knuckle without much effort.

"You wanna get fucked, don't you, kid? You wanna come

with my big cock in your tight ass?"

"God, yes, Frank. I want you to fuck me. Please, fuck my ass."

"Wow, didn't have any trouble that time, did you, kid?"

I watched him cross the room and dig in his desk drawer. He had taken off his boxers, and his hard cock was jutting straight out in front of him. It was bigger than any I had ever seen before, and my own cock hardened at the prospect. He returned to the bed, grabbing me by the hips and moving me forward. I heard the pop of the lube top opening, and soon the warm press of his tongue was traded for the cool slide of his lubed fingers. He was patient, working me open a bit at a time with his sawing fingers. My discomfort faded fast, replaced with deep need. Just as I got used to his intrusion, he was gone.

I heard the crinkle of the foil condom wrapper, and I held my breath waiting for him to roll it on. The unyielding press of his cock against my asshole forced me to breathe again. Frank gasped right along with me when I felt my sphincter give way and let him in fully. The fingers that had been digging bruises into my hips released, the pain only making my cock swell more in my stroking hand. I knew I wouldn't last long, and when he started moving inside my ass in deep, measured strokes, I cried out louder than I intended to. He wanted me to feel every inch, taking his time to pull almost all the way out before plunging back in to the root. I squeezed my eyes shut, perspiration dampening my face and back as I took him. Frank threw gasoline on my fire with more dirty words.

"That's it. Jerk that fucking cock, kid. I want you to come and squeeze that ass around my dick. Come hard for me, Andrew."

I moved my hips mindlessly back toward him, the way he said my name burning a hole in my brain. Among all the filthy, dirty things that came out of his mouth, his saying my name had the biggest effect on me. My dick twitched in my hand, come spurting hot and sticky from the tip, and my ass contracted around Frank's cock, just like he wanted. My head flew back, my moans and screams bouncing off the metal and paneled walls. Frank was pounding me with more fury and force than even my fantasies had allowed. I felt his sweat dripping onto my back, and as I milked the last drops from my dick, Frank drove into me to the hilt, his thick chest collapsing onto my back as he came violently behind me. My knees gave way, leaving only my elbows to hold us both up on the bed. His teeth sank into my shoulder as the last quakes rumbled through him, his panting breath hot on my already soaked skin.

He rolled away, tossing the condom into a nearby trash can before covering us both with the standard-issue green base blanket crammed into the corner of his bed. I didn't dare look at him, but that lasted a few seconds, until Frank pressed a hand to my cheek and turned me toward him. I expected awkward words, but the only thing that passed between us at that moment was the sweetest kiss I ever had. Frank pulled back and smiled, a silent chuckle shaking us both in his bed.

"What's so funny?"

"I just hope you don't get fired, kid."

"They fire people for fucking down here? Then how do you still have a job?"

"That's not what I meant, smartass. I just hope the lab doesn't mind. Because I get the feeling you are going to be very, very distracted from now on."

"I hope so. After all, someone told me that everyone needs a good distraction."

Frank laughed again.

"Good? I'd say it was a pretty fucking great distraction."

# BACK ROOM BUDDIES AT THE RUSTY SCREW

Jeff Funk

A feller at the bar last night called me a whore. He wasn't kiddin' around either. This fucker meant it. I have to say, it kind of hurt my feelings. I'm not that slutty, am I? I used to be a good boy, old-fashioned and all, and I tried to date men proper. I would take 'em out for dinner or a movie before I fucked their brains out. But when money got tight, and all of that wining and dining wasn't an option, I found a more economical solution for tending to my needs.

The place was called the Rusty Screw. It was a leather bar, down by the old abandoned cheese factory along the St. Mary's river. The owner named it after his favorite drink. He liked the dirty sounding beverages. When he ordered a shot, his usual choice was a "cowboy cocksucker," but that wouldn't look so snappy in the Yellow Pages, now would it? Before the Screw opened, there was only one other club in town for men of my ilk. Only problem was, it was full of scrawny lads who mostly worked in the shopping mall. They dressed funny and talked like girls, nasty ones at that. I didn't see a single fella there who caused my dick to chub up. I was a man, damn it. And I wanted to get with another man. Why was that so complicated?

I didn't have that problem at the Rusty Screw. This was a man's bar, all right, with blue-collar types. There was hardly a clean-shaven face among 'em. They all had beards, moustaches, goatees or dark whiskers—at least a couple days' worth of scruff. These were factory workers gettin' off from second shift and construction workers wantin' to blow off a little steam. Or more aptly, shoot a big load. See, unlike the frilly bar on Sallee Street, this joint had a naughty back room, and there was more than gropin' through jeans going on, lemme tell ya.

The first time I messed around back there, it was 'cause this butch plumber with a buzz cut came up and pinched my nipples god-awful hard. Pissed me off, in fact. I thought, hell, if you're gonna sample the wares, I'll sample 'em right back. So I grabbed the waistband of his jeans, pushed a paw inside past his underwear and helped myself to a heapin' handful of his junk. I was gonna teach him a lesson, maybe give his nuts an equally vicious squeeze. But then he let out this low grunt—"Oh"—as if he were mighty pleased by my firm grip. Suddenly, I wasn't mad no more; I was horned up. I could feel his meat fighting against its trapped position. I loosened my fingers. Right quickly, it grew to man-sized proportions. I fiddled with his fly and eased his piece outta there to see what we were talkin' about. What I had before me was quite possibly the prettiest pecker I'd ever laid eyes on.

*Do I dare suck this thing out in public view?* There were other men standin' around, but most of them ignored us. A couple of horny rednecks were watching with interest though. *Aw, fuck it. I'm gonna go for it,* I thought. Blow jobs weren't exactly unheard of in the back room. I dropped to my knees. The rednecks moseyed over to witness the dirty shenanigans. Their huddled stance blocked the view of casual observers, giving us a bit of privacy. Mighty nice of 'em. I was much obliged.

With my left hand, I held the plumber's nuts firmly in place. Then I gulped his peter, chowin' on it till it slid down my throat and choked me but good. Brought tears to my eyes, as a matter of fact, but did that make my enthusiasm wane? Hell, nope. I tried 'er again. This time, I swallowed it whole until my nose was buried in his bush. The way he growled and carried on let me know that he enjoyed the hell out of gettin' an inside tour of my esophagus.

I had a good amount of spit worked up, enough to grease the way for him to fuck my face silly. He grabbed hold of my head and went to town, rocking his hips. I noticed that his fingernails had dirt under 'em. I love it when a bruiser manhandles me and takes what he wants. His cock popped out of my mouth with a wet smack. He took matters in hand, workin' that well-slobbered member like he was milkin' a cow's teat. His fist twisted and jacked. Must've been the type of guy who needed his own manual stimulation to get off. His brown eyes glazed over with ornery lust. His smile turned sly. Gettin' close, I could tell.

"Come on, man. Let it go," I said. Then I stuck out my tongue as far as I could to give him a target to shoot for.

Bull's-eye.

*Mmm, good and salty. Just the way I like it.* I didn't waste a drop. I took everything he had till his nuts were drained. It was odd, knowing that his load was goin' down the hatch and mixing with beer only, not a belly full of dinner that I'd gone and paid for, for the both of us. Naw, this guy had bought his *own* drinks. Imagine that! Fuck that datin' crap. Cheap was the way to go, I decided. And boy howdy, was I hooked on having easy access to rough and rowdy men.

Let me fill you in on somethin'. Looky here, what Joe citizen types don't understand is, if you've been convicted of a felony there ain't a helluva lotta places that'll hire ya. But now, construction crews are a little less picky. Contractors don't give a shit if you got caught with more than two ounces of weed, or beat up somebody who probably had it comin'. They need a man's man. Fellers who've picked up a muscle or two over the years and can handle heavy machinery, operate large vehicles and not get knocked to the ground by the power of a jackhammer. Whenever I'd get a glimpse of inked flesh in the Rusty Screw, you can damn bet it wasn't one of those tribal armbands folks get from a shop in the hippie part of town. No, sir. Them there was *prison* tattoos.

Speaking of guys who looked like they were in prison, this one rough character with a ponytail and a scar across his face once said to me, "It's been so long since I've had a blow job. I don't suppose you'd give me one, would ya?"

I scratched my chin whiskers, pondering the notion. Then I said, "Nope!"

I'm funny. If a guy asks me for a blow job, I usually won't give him one. It's shitty of me, I know. But that's how I feel. Givin' oral has to be my choice, tickle *my* fancy. Maybe if he hadn't been unsure of himself, he'd have gotten what he wanted. I reckon if he would've acted like he had every right in the world to squirt his cum down my throat, I probably would have gotten off on it. Sometimes, it's more fun if they *don't* want their dicks sucked. Then I'll try to trick 'em into it. I'll tell ya who's a master at that maneuver.

Ole Johnny.

This weasely little guy has managed to get my cock in his mouth more times than I care to admit. One time, I was seeing a good-lookin' jock type, and I was adamant that Johnny not slurp my wiener.

I said, "Don't you suck that dick, Johnny. I'm datin' someone now and I'm tryin' to be proper…so just jack me off."

"I won't," Johnny said. "I won't suck it."

He sucked it. He was right sneaky about it, too. He was strokin' away, and it was feelin' mighty nice. Then he gave the head of my peter a random lick. I spoke the Lord's name and let out a hot sigh. He took that as a go-ahead, and before I could stop him, his head was bobbin' away. *Damn it,* I thought. *Another secret to keep from Charles.* So much for my resolve. He was damn good at it though. Why deny myself the pleasure of one of Johnny's trademark blow jobs? That single-minded, scrawny little fucker. Bless his heart.

Let that be a lesson to you folks. If you're ever wantin' a hearty blow job outta me, you're better off sayin' something like, "Well, now goddamn, Jake. Don't you suck my pride and joy, ya hear?"

Oh, I won't. Scout's honor.

Ernie was a bricklayer who might've actually been straight— or straighter than most. He rattled on and on about women the whole time I was servicin' him. The harder I sucked, the faster he talked about all them titties and pussies. Kind of funny, really. I figured it was my goal to get him speakin' in tongues. Or hell, start bid-callin' like a goddamn auctioneer: "I got pussy goin' for five! Who'll give me five-dollar-five-dollar-five-dollar pussy? Now ten!" A real motormouth, this fella. Pussy, pussy, pussy. To some guys, that ramblin' might've been annoying, but I took it that I was doin' a good job. Besides, ain't suckin' straight dick always considered a delicacy? And what he had between his legs, shoo-doggie. He could put somebody in the hospital with that thing if he weren't careful. But most naughty boys love a good challenge, don't they?

I'll let you in on a little secret: some of these older guys are packin' the biggest tools. I ain't lying. Occasionally, I'll throw 'em a bone. I figure, when I'm in my senior years, I'll still be wantin' me some action. Hopefully, there'll be a fine, strappin' stud who'll do the same for me, ya know? This one time, I fooled around with a distinguished, silver-haired daddy. As I undid his Sansabelt pants, I said, "Let's see whatcha got in there." I pulled that monster out and shouted, "Holy fuckin' shit, old-timer! You're packin' a blue racer in them trousers." It didn't get all the way erect, but it sure was fun to play with. And the best part? This guy *appreciated* it. I was smilin' big and proud that I could do a good deed for him.

The oldest duck I ever fucked around with was an eighty-eight-year-old pipe organist, who went at my organ like he was playin' a Bach fugue. He had a bit of a shake to his hand that felt dandy to me. It was a tender touch, the likes of which I'd never experienced before. He kept saying, "My gawd. You're so hard."

Ever respectful of my elders, I said, "Yes, sir. It sure is."

"Gawd sakes, it's just so *hard*." He examined my turgid manhood further. "I could get like this in my younger years. Been a long time though." He emitted a raspy chuckle. "All I can tell ya is enjoy it while ya can."

"Oh, I intend to," I said.

While he was having his fun, this younger guy joined us. Now this dude wasn't the best lookin' guy I've ever had; in fact, he made me think of the old expression "uglier than a mud fence." But ya know what? Ugly guys are pretty fuckin' good at sex. He was sorta lumpy lookin' and he had badly calloused hands. That particular skin texture struck a sharp contrast to the baby softness of my freshly shaved scrotal flesh. He made me *jump* when he first cupped my balls. What the hell did he do for a living? Felt like he went out and chopped wood all day long.

So it was the old duffer pullin' on my pole, and Mud Fence, with his calloused hands, needlin' my nuts. The old man squatted to get a good gander. Just then, I blasted my jizz all over his cardigan sweater, really hosed it down. A few spurts landed on Mud Fence's boots. Damn, that was a good nut.

Later, I was whistlin' to myself as I left the Screw. The wind had picked up, causing the trees by the river to rustle and sway. The leaves were upturned and silvery. It looked like rain. A black pickup was goin' slowly alongside me as my work boots crunched along the gravel path. I didn't think nothin' of it, a cruiser probably. Hell, there were always school principals runnin' around back there. Ministers, husbands—all sorts of sneaky fuckers—were on the prowl for dick. I fired up the LeSabre and got a few blocks away. At a stoplight, I noticed that same black truck. And the driver? Why goddamn, it was ole Mud Fence. He must've really enjoyed hisself back there and didn't want the fun to end.

The light turned green, and I stomped the gas. Now I live in Auburn, Indiana, a good twenty miles from Fort Wayne. Surely, he wouldn't drive all that way. He wasn't that hard up, was he?

I pulled onto I-69, the interstate that's a straight shot to Auburn. By god, so did Mud Fence. No matter how fast or slow I went, he stayed right behind me. The longer I drove, the worse I worried. He must have a screw loose, stalkin' me like this, right? In the rearview mirror, those low beams shinin' in the rain seemed menacing. What if this guy was dangerous? Did he ever serve time in the pokey? I sure as hell wasn't gonna lead him to my house. *If I have to,* I thought, *I'll go to the police station and start honkin' my horn.*

When I got to town, I pulled into Taco Bell just to shake him. There was quite a line at the drive-through, folks like myself getting back from the Fort Wayne bars. Unlike me, though, most of them were probably coming from the strip joints. Fort Wayne's full of titty bars and churches; the two go hand in hand, or so I gather. The line was moving slower than hell, as usual.

Through my cracked windshield, I watched him circle the restaurant's parking lot. Then he took a second lap. He slowed down when he got to me. I shook my head at the lumpy silhouette in the truck's cab. Suddenly, I heard his muffler pop like firecrackers. With an angry burst of speed, he tore out of there and turned to get back onto the interstate.

Probably wanted his dick sucked. *Sorry, pal. Not tonight. I got a bean burrito with my name on it. But maybe next time.*

This one guy I messed around with worked in a steel mill. He told me that he had metal shavings embedded in his hands. I worried what would happen if he jacked me off. My johnson's generally hard as steel, but I didn't want steel stuck in it. However, his *mouth* was in fine workin' order. I mentioned this fact, to which he replied, "I'll suck you off if you wear a condom."

"Well, all right...you won't taste nothin' though. Ya sure that's how ya wanna go?"

He was sure.

Steel guy went to work, slobberin' on that rubber. His lips were tight with extra suction so I could feel somethin'. And damn if it wasn't one of the best suck jobs of my life. When I was ready to shoot, he pulled a trick with his mouth. To this day, I'm not sure what the hell he did. Must be some sort of fellatio technique that can only be done when your hog's trapped in latex. I filled that fuckin' thing so full of gravy, I'm surprised it didn't come squirtin' out the bottom. Shee-it! I took to buyin' mint-flavored rubbers so I wouldn't miss out on his fine oral skills the next time our paths crossed.

I used to play a game with a guy named Jeremiah. We had set

up the rules while chatting online. Okay, I would be sitting on a bar stool, tucked back in one of the cruise stalls with my pants unzipped and my T-shirt hanging down over my lap. When Jeremiah arrived, he would stomp right up to me, reach in and help himself to my boner. I was powerless to use my hands. He had full control. It was up to him to hide me away or show me off to whomever he felt like. Jeremiah said, "I don't have one dick; I have *two* dicks, to do with as I please. Mine and yours." Sometimes a good lookin' fella would wander into the back room, and Jeremiah would whisper dirty things into my ear, like, "What if I told that guy he could come over and do anything he wanted to you, anything at all and that you wouldn't stop him?" He said the same thing a couple times about fellas he knew I wouldn't want to mess around with. I just sat on my hands. Couldn't use 'em, couldn't get up and leave.

Most of the time, he stood there sipping his drink while his other hand was deep inside my jeans, holding on to me like a dog leash. Whenever my dick pulsed, he'd give it a squeeze. It seemed like I could feel a heartbeat in my hard-on, with his hand wrapped around it so tight. I tell you, I was *rock* hard. Involuntarily, it would throb. Another squeeze.

On we went, playing that game for hours. I liked having him in charge like that. He took good care of me. I miss that man's dirty mind. So often, the good ones drift out of your life without a word of good-bye.

Henry was another kinky fucker. He was a brawny blond with a thick brown beard, who drove a concrete truck for a living. He told me that this fella he played with liked to whip his dick. It was probably no more than a miniflogger or something pretty tame. Naturally, I pictured a nasty master, standing ten paces away with a bullwhip, givin' his peter a fierce lashing. At work, he liked to wear ball-weights inside his dusty jeans while he was around the other members of the crew. He got off, knowing that those straight boys were oblivious to his private plight. That's one way to keep the job site interesting, eh? He sure was into torturin' hisself, I guess.

Group sex could break out in the back room at any given time, but it usually happened on slow nights. Thursdays were good. In the front bar, they were busy ruinin' my memories of some of my favorite songs. Karaoke, they called it. Some of that bellerin' got the dogs howlin' in the neighborhood. The *really* bad singers sent guys runnin' for the back room, where they would often stumble upon a blue-collar game of Twister. More than likely, you'd find me in the middle of it.

On one chilly night in October, there were more than eight of us goin' at it. I was on my knees, suckin' a thick log that belonged to a tall carpenter named Paul. There was Johnny on his belly, arching his neck to wet my works. Did I tell ya he was missing most of his front teeth? At least I didn't have to worry about him scrapin' my cockhead. Behind my ass was a beefy bear on the floor, lying on his back to get at my nuts and tongue my hole whenever I'd sit on his face. Add to that a guy a piece on both of my nipples, twistin' away like they were dialing for a Canadian radio station on a shortwave. Peeper types were watchin'. Freddy and Max seemed to be waitin' for a new configuration to break out so they could get their turn. A couple of farm boys were reachin' in to grope any manly parts that were left untended or plug their fingers into orifices that needed it.

I was known as a big shooter. I was sort of a legend at the bar. Folks liked to watch to see how far I could squirt. I started gruntin' loudly to let the room know that I was gettin' there.

Randy said, "Oh, he's about to come? Hold on, lemme in there to do the nut pull!"

The nut pull. Shoo, that's a good one. When you're fixin'

to unleash your seed, your nuts will want to pull up closer to your body. It's just nature. But the fun thing to do with 'em is, wait until they start their ascent. Then right as you're shootin' you'll wanna have a buddy give them a solid yank back down. As if to say, "Whoa, boys. Where do you think *you're* goin'?" You know that sensation when you accidentally touch an electric fence, how it makes you feel like you've got water runnin' in your veins? This is pretty close to that, only it's your balls that get all squirmy on ya. Try it sometime. It'll make ya shoot buckets, like I did—all over Mike MacDonald's leather jacket, in this case.

Tell me, does that sound like the makings of a whore? A *whore*? Naw, I'm just regular. Doin' what anyone would do. If you were in the back room, you wouldn't be sitting there with your hands folded on your knee like you were posing for a church portrait, would ya? Hell no. I'm willin' to bet you'd grab ya some cock. As for that bitter feller who squinted his eyes and tried to stick me with that label? Maybe he's still sore 'cause he asked me for a blow job a while back. Asked me for one! Well, of course, I turned him down. I reckon he's still scratchin' his head. But I ain't that hard to figure out, now am I?

# THE HYPHENATED HANDYMAN

Rob Rosen

The project was seemingly easy enough: a larger deck out back, a bit of landscaping, a couple of days' work, tops. *Tops* being the optimal word here. But wait, I'll get to that. See, I might've been able to do the job myself, but, well, two left hands made for one miserable deck. In other words, I let my fingers do the walking, dialing a local contractor who had gotten rave reviews on Yelp, strangely all from men. Though that little mystery was solved in due time, as well.

His name was Lou, and he was available the next morning for a look-see, followed by an estimate, hopefully within my price range. I pictured a middle-aged man, pot-bellied, messy-haired, muddy-booted, cigar-smoking, über-straight dude. What I got instead was a whole other list of hyphenated words, none of which tallied up to straight, über or otherwise. Lou was superhot, mighty-fine, white-toothed, perfect-complexioned and if the snug, scissor-cut denim shorts and ultratight pink polo were any indication, dude was anything but straight. And, yes, he merited even more hyphens, but my lust-addled brain had temporarily shut down upon first glimpse of him.

"Jim. Jim, um, Gates," I offered, sweaty hand in his big, strong, meaty one, flesh on flesh, a jolt of electricity riding shotgun up and down my spine.

"Lou," he said, though, of course, I already knew that. Still, it made the handshake last a few milliseconds longer, so *no problemo*. "Now, let's see this little deck of yours."

I inhaled sharply, a bead of sweat suddenly trickling down my forehead. "Excuse me?"

He played with his honey-wheat-colored goatee, and reiterated, "Your deck. The reason I'm here, right?"

"Oh, my *deck*. Yes, sorry, I thought you said...um, never mind. It's out back. Follow me." I sighed, trying my darndest to collect my wits. Trying and failing, mind you. Out back, the sun shining down on him, eyes the color of a perfect, cloudless summer sky, pecs a'poppin', nipples, er, a'nipplin', it was all I could do to still formulate words. "See for yourself," I told him, pointing out my dilemma. "It only holds two, right now. I'd like it to seat six, comfortably. And the landscape around it needs a proper fixer-up, too. It came this way when I bought the place." Emphasis on the *came*, and his eyes were suddenly glued to mine, an eddy of adrenaline swirling like a tempest in my belly.

"Easy as pie," he replied, after a quick once-over, neck moving up and down. "I can do it myself. How about this weekend?" Then he named his price. Heck, I would've paid *him* just to show up. In other words, we had a deal. "How about eight on Saturday?" he suggested.

I chuckled, knowing how unlikely it was I'd be up at eight on a Saturday morning. "How about you let yourself in the side gate?"

We shook hands again, his as clammy as my own this go

around. Bing-fucking-o. Still, it was only Monday, and Saturday was forever away. Meaning, that weekend morning, I woke up, slipped on a pair of shorts, skimpy at best, brewed a fresh pot, and took my coffee al fresco, completely forgetting why, who, when and what the fuck was going on.

"Ah!" I squealed, just a tad on the girlish side—a smidge, really. But a shirtless Adonis bent over, crack unfurled; well, it was more than I was expecting so early in the morning. Just a tad. Just a smidge. Until he jumped up and I got a good look at his ripped, hairy chest and washboard abs, a happy, blond love-trail zooming down to points yet unknown, that tad/smidge thing of mine exploding to big, heaping handful proportions. "Oh, it's just you, Lou," I said, exhaling, hand over furiously pumping heart.

"Nice to see you, too, Jim," he replied, with a smirk. "That coffee of yours have a twin?"

I regained my composure, almost, and said, "Sure. Cream and sugar?"

"Lots of cream, sugar," he replied, with a wink, a mad samba beating out in my chest yet again, a *boing* stirring in my already too tight shorts.

"Coming right up," said I, quickly turning, eyelids fluttering, as I went to retrieve his cup of java, returning to find him sitting and waiting, legs spread wide, tight denim jeans hiding little, torso sweat-soaked, face still angelic, wink ever present. I set both cups down, nearly spilling half of the hot liquid on the ground below, then joined him, chairs facing, uncomfortable in my near-nakedness, though rightfully glad for his.

"Already got a good start," he said, taking his first sip. "Should be finished by midday tomorrow at the latest. If..." Another sip followed by a lengthy pause.

"If?"

A red flush spread across his stubbled, chiseled cheeks, his eyes temporarily aimed downward, package-level. "Yeah, um, if I'm not *distracted*." He raised his hand and pointed his index finger at my crotch, swirling said digit around in loops.

I craned my neck down to find one of my balls hanging out, dangling low, eager to say its good mornings. I quickly tucked it back in, my own face burning red as hot coals now. "Uh, oops," I coughed out. I glanced back up; he was smiling, devilishly, beguilingly.

"See, distracting," he repeated, scratching his head, the grin going northward.

Then a new thought for me, an upping of the ante, so to speak. "Ah, so, what you're saying is, you'll have to be here longer if you're, uh, distracted, right?"

He touched finger to nose. "Exactly."

I stood up and set my coffee cup down, thumbs tucked into my shorts, the material pushed lower just an inch, my trimmed bush making an appearance. "Distracting?"

"You just added at least an hour, boss."

Another inch, the base of my shaft exposed, then half of my already arcing cock. "And this? At least a couple more, right?"

His hand was on his crotch now, pushing down, prodding the lump. "Oh, at least."

I slid out of the shorts, dropping them to the ground and kicking them off, my cock thick and rigid, jutting straight out, maxing to its full seven inches, a shiny bead of precome dripping over the pulsing tip. "Guess I'm pushing three days now, huh?" I gave it a tug and a stroke, a soft moan escaping from between my lips. "How many days would it take if we're both naked?"

He answered my question with one of his own. "Didn't anyone ever tell you you're not supposed to hit on the hired help?" He stood, the top button of his jeans undone. He was obviously going commando, his blond bush wondrously in view, golden in the early morning light.

"If they did, it's only because they never got a gander at you." I moved in, two feet in front of him, one, my breathing shallow.

"And what's good for the goose..." He reached out, stroking my chest, tweaking a stiff nipple, a twist, a pull, a massive groan let out by yours truly. The jeans were dropped, his cock bouncing out, shorter than mine by an inch, thicker than mine by the same, the head like a nice-sized plum, giant swaying balls, haloed in a ring of curly blond hair, legs akin to tree trunks, well-worked calves all trimmed in the same wonderful blond.

I mimicked his finger-to-nose move. "Exactly." The gap was closed, and his arms were around my waist, mine around his, hands roaming north and south, east and west and all points in between—mostly the between. Lips like magnets, joined together, parting, tongues colliding, thrashing: it was heaven on a beautiful Saturday morning. *Fuck the deck.*

He moved his mouth away, beelining it up my neck, a million goose bumps rising in his wake before he landed on my ear for a suck and a slurp and a tender bite. "I think we just hit those three days, boss."

"Couldn't care less, Mister Contractor," said I, sinking to my knees, slapping his cock against my lips, licking the salty jizz off the head, then downing him in one fell swoop, a happy gagging tear cascading down my cheek as his prick pushed down my throat. I tickled his heavy balls, then gave a tug, his legs instantly buckling.

"Play nice," he moaned.

"Nice is for Boy Scouts." I pulled him down on the ground with me. "And we know how they feel about perverts like us."

Again the kiss, our bodies leaning, falling, rolling in the cool grass. "Guess we can form our own troop, then."

That idea I liked, a lot. I flipped him over on his back, my body on his, on top, as promised, though not topping, not yet. His hands were held above his head, my face just over his, eyes locked, watching, waiting, our cocks grinding together, sweat-lubed. I moved my face lower down, mouth on a proffered nipple for a gnash. He arched his back, moaning loudly, the sound swirling around us, shaming the crickets.

I let go of his hands, mouth going south, tongue rolling over peaks and valleys, a joyous giggle rising from him when I swirled around and around his sweat-pooled belly button. Then I moved lower still, through a mound of sun-kissed blond hair, his legs lifted up, bent at the knee, heels on my shoulders, his beautiful, pink, crinkled hole winking up at me.

I dove in for a lick and a slurp that was salty, musky, like ambrosia, my tongue poking its way inside of him, his ass shoving into my face while he began a slow stroke on his thick prick. I glanced up, his balls bouncing an inch away, miles of flawless tanned skin stretching up my line of vision, his face tilted down, eyes on the action, a wink and a smirk that sent my tummy rumbling, my tongue replaced by a spit-slick index finger.

His eyelids closed for the briefest of moments, and he gave a sharp inhale, and clenched around my impaled digit. A count of three, pleasure and pain obviously giving way to the former, and then he picked up the pace on his dick, eyes open again, pools of blue on a hot summer's day. A second finger got shoved deep, deep inside, my free hand now working my slick tool, both of us in sync as I added a third finger to the mix.

"Dirty, dirty man," he panted.

"Thank goodness for showers," quipped I. *And hot contractors.*

His balls began a steady climb, my fingers suddenly butting

up against granite, the telltale tingle rising up my spine. "Close," he groaned, the word reverberating inside my head.

"Closer," I amended, retracting my hand from his ass as I knelt over him, balls banging against balls, both our hands jerking like crazy now, eyes locked, his on my dick, mine on his.

He shot a split second before I did, his whole body quivering like a newly fired arrow, his cock spewing thick torrents of come that fired out and splattered down, a blanket of white against all that glorious tan, his moans and groans matching mine. Then it was my turn, shooting blast after blast of spunk, my legs quaking, head thrown back, my hefty load mixing with his before it spilled over his sides, my body collapsing on top of his, two sticky messes, lips again joined as one.

Soon enough, though, we were up and getting dressed, him going back to work, me, peeping Jim that I am, ogling him from between venetian blinds, my deck growing and growing with each passing minute, cock growing, too, every time I replayed the scene in my head. Hours later, I ran out of the house to do some errands; when I returned, he was gone, just a note in his stead: *Tomorrow morning, boss. Thinking of some nifty distractions already.* As was I, of course.

It being Sunday, I awoke the next morning even later, the sound of hammering pounding away in my head. I poked my face out the window, shouting, "Are you fucking kidding me?"

The pounding stopped, ever so briefly. "Kidding, no," he yelled. "*Fucking* is optional."

"Ah," said I, my dick springing to life. "No wonder you've got five stars on Yelp."

"Nope," he hollered, hammer again striking nail. "Only you get that option. It's thrown in for free. For running behind and all." Some more racket followed, then, "Come check on me in a few hours, otherwise this fucker will never get finished."

All I heard was *come* and *fuck*. Still, I got his point, retreating to the farthest and quietest reaches of my abode, biding my time. And biding while fully erect is never very enjoyable.

When the noise ceased a long while later, I emerged from my seclusion, naked and swaying into my backyard. The deck was done: huge, perfect and beautiful. Same thing could be said for Lou, who was also naked, prone, ass up in the air, with a bottle of lube by his side, a rubber right next to it.

"Now that's service," I said, with a long whistle, jogging over and bending down for an eager kiss and a jack on his steely rod.

"With a smile," he added. "Now fuck me, boss."

Needless to say, he didn't have to tell me twice. Heck, he didn't have to tell me at all; it was all I'd been thinking about since I laid eyes on him. Meaning, I was sheathed and lubed in no time flat. And here, of course, is that long-awaited topping I promised.

Gently, slowly, tenderly, I popped my dickhead inside, eliciting a quick inhale from him, a sharp exhale from me, and then there were a million volts of adrenaline zooming down my spine and out my cock, every nerve ending in my body on fire as I filled him up, inch by throbbing inch, until my balls were lapping up against his fleshy shores. He looked up and grinned, his hands around the back of my neck, pulling me down for a deep soul kiss while I eased my dick back out, then shoved it back in, out and in, slowly but steadily gaining speed, both of us panting inside each other's mouths, sweat gliding off of me and onto him.

Minutes later, I was rocketing my cock inside of him, his ass shoving up to meet each of my thrusts, grunts and groans ricocheting off the fence that surrounded us, playing like a symphony inside my head.

"Man, you feel good," I whispered into his mouth.

"Ditto," he whispered back. "Now let's give this deck a good fucking christening."

"Emphasis on the fucking."

Which is exactly what we did, his hand moving lightning fast on his prick, my cock pulverizing his hole, both of our bodies moving as one, until I didn't know where he ended and I began. I stared deep into his eyes that were sparkling like sapphires, and nodded when I was close.

"Let 'er rip," he growled.

So I kicked it into overdrive, piston-fucking his ass like there was no tomorrow, until I filled that rubber up with ounce after creamy, hot ounce of come, and his cock shot so much spunk that I was certain the next three times he had sex his well would run completely dry. Then, as I'd done the day before, I collapsed on top of him, gasping for breath, sticking to him in a mess of sweat and jizz.

"Nice fucking deck," I eventually panted. "But the landscaping isn't done yet."

He chuckled. "Tomorrow, boss. Tomorrow."

Tomorrow was a workday for me. In fact, I was up and out the door before he ever arrived, my stomach sinking when I hopped outside, naked and hard and utterly alone. Still, I had to admit my deck looked glorious, gorgeous wood, big enough to fit a small crowd, even when it was just one other certain person I wanted to keep company with right about then.

It was then I spotted it, a note taped to a middle board: *Will be finished by the time you get home, boss. Thanks for the distractions. Enjoy!*

"Sure, no problem," I sighed, trudging off to work.

I got home late, the sun already sinking into the horizon. I started heading for my front door when I noticed a glow in my backyard, so I headed through the gate instead, my heart stopping for the briefest of seconds when I spotted it, him, every-thing.

"Ta-da!" he shouted, dressed in his finest work overalls and nothing much else, a smile big and bright and wide plastered to his handsome face.

The landscaping was stunning: new grass, flowers, shrubs, all trimmed, all edged to perfection. Though this was not what had made me suck in my breath, not by a long shot. And let me tell you, I'd had enough long shots over the last couple of days to know. See, the deck, my beautiful deck, was festooned with candles, all lit, glowing like a million fireflies, with a table dead center, two chairs pulled out, a stunning bouquet of roses, and dinner waiting.

I smiled and met him halfway. "Um, wow," I managed.

"You like?" he asked, arms outstretched, a soft kiss for yours truly. "Not too over the top?"

"It's perfect," I replied, arms wrapped around him, my head nuzzled in his neck. "All mine?"

He laughed and held on tight. "All yours, boss." He gave me another kiss, then another.

I mirrored the kiss and the hug, melting into him, my deck twinkling like the stars up above. Mine. All mine. No hyphens needed. That one word was plenty all by itself.

# CUM-SLAMMING HANDYMAN

**Bearmuffin**

was in the shower when Bart Harris knocked on my door. I'd advertised in the local paper for a handyman to work on my dude ranch twenty-five miles west of Galveston, Texas. I had plenty of lusty cowpokes to round up my cattle, but I needed a stud to do the painting and other maintenance tasks. I got out of the shower, wrapped a towel around my waist and answered the door. And there he was, the ideal stud in every respect: a big six-foot-three tower of manly muscle right at my doorstep.

I immediately noted his blue eyes and that he was packing a big piece of meat down there below his belt. I just couldn't keep my eyes off it. Bart was somewhere in his early twenties. "I saw the ad in the paper," he said with an irresistible, soft, Southern drawl. "Figured what the hell, I'd give it a shot." When I asked him if he had any experience he just shook his head. "Nah, I just got outta prison." His words felt like a fist slamming into my solar plexus. I took a good look at his rugged face stubbled with four or five days' growth of beard. And then I remembered. It had been front-page news a few years ago.

Bart had been a lead rider in the local rodeo but as fate would have it he got mixed up with the wrong crowd and one thing lead to another. He eventually wound up in prison for armed robbery. The man had nerve, that's for sure! I took one good look at him and had to admit that I was impressed by his size, bulk and attitude. More than that, he projected a powerful physical allure. His manly smell collected in my nostrils.

Bart had shaggy straw-colored hair and a thick moustache. He was wearing tight, faded Wranglers, a Stetson and a tight, red button-up shirt. His collar was open and a golden tuft of hair at the base of his throat implied a thicker fleece on his body. And though Bart seemed to be a true and blue cowboy, he easily reminded me of a Viking warrior, one of that gang of bold, hearty and wild men who ravaged, pillaged and plundered and took their pleasure wherever and whenever they could find it. He was so big that he had to turn sideways to get inside. He sprawled out on my couch and I offered him a beer, which he accepted with thanks.

I wondered if he noticed the subtle look of apprehension on my face that I was trying so hard to disguise as he told me of his life in prison. And while he spoke I could not keep my eyes off his bulging crotch. His legs were spread wide affording me a perfect glimpse of a menacing bulge and making me wonder if he just had a big dick when soft or was it throbbing and ready for action. I glanced at his big hands with their long, thick fingers and wondered what they would feel like on my body, my chest, my nipples.

He finished off his beer, crumpled the empty can in his paw and dropped it on the ground. I got up and got him another beer and suddenly noticed the thick smell of testosterone lingering in the air, a deep, rich odor that I recognized as his smell. It was powerful, intoxicating and lust arousing!

He grabbed the new beer, popped it open and took a drink. He said that he had kept himself in shape by working out with weights. That's when a particular train of thought started. Somehow, I'd get a full display of his magnificent physique. I gave him a job.

I told him to start painting the house. He followed me out to the garage where I showed him the paints and brushes. I gave him some white overalls that I hoped would fit him and a baseball cap, since I didn't have a painter's cap. He painted for hours until lunchtime, and that's when I went outside to invite him to join me and the rest of the men for chow.

I stopped in my tracks. My jaw hit the dirt. There he was working in his briefs. It was a particularly hot summer day anyway, so I figured what the hell. Just as I'd hoped I had a perfect view of his magnificent body. I homed in on his swollen, meaty nipples, and I wanted to suck on them. I certainly was aroused by the sight of his butt. He had nice, big, bubble buns, just like a football player. My eyes roamed over his hairy body, the baseball-sized biceps, the broad shoulders, the pumped-up pecs and lean set of solid abs. His whole body was just begging to be worshipped!

Watching him work in those tight, white briefs excited me beyond all reason. My cock began to rise and stiffen at the unexpected and magnificent sight of this hairy man working in his underwear in the hot summer sun. My tongue itched with a lusty craving as I tried to imagine what his sweat would taste like —it was running down in thick streams over his muscles. I wanted to make love to his sweaty ass, to worship his butthole for hours, my tongue working inside it like a washing machine.

His thick legs were planted wide apart so I could get a good look at his swinging cock and balls jiggling inside his white briefs. I watched his massive frame as he worked, grunting and groaning. His briefs were almost transparent with sweat. I loved the way the briefs clung to his big, beefy buttocks.

I went up to him, mesmerized by the astonishing sight of this handsome, hairy man wearing nothing but a baseball cap and white cotton briefs, holding a huge paintbrush in one hand and painting my house as if it were the most natural thing in the world. I stood in front of the ladder in silent, worshipful wonder.

He suddenly noticed me and grunted and smiled down at me, and I noticed that his half-hard cock was sticking out through the pee-flap. My mouth dropped open again and I was transfixed, rooted to the spot, my eyes glued to the thickness and size of his cock, which was circled with blue veins. "The overalls didn't fit," he said. "I don't want to get paint on my jeans." But I barely paid attention to what he was saying, as all I could do was look at his cock. And then the smell of his unwashed cock drifted to me, a smell so pungent, meaty and extremely arousing that I couldn't help myself. I had to jack off. I slid my hand to my bulging crotch, squeezed it and then began to unbutton my jeans to free my lust-aroused cock.

But Bart beat me to it. He began masturbating, pointing the head of his cock at my face. He looked deep into my eyes and that look of recognition passed between us, that promise of revelation when two men know that one is about to suck the other's cock.

I greedily stuck my face under his balls. Now I was smothered in his mighty low-danglers. The smell of his ripe, potent balls was wonderful, dilating my nostrils and making me dizzy with lust. I nestled my face against his balls for a while to enjoy their warmth, their musky odor.

I felt Bart's hand on my head. "My cock," he drawled. "Suck my cock!"

I glanced at Bart's spasming meat and grinned, marveling at the thick shaft latticed with crisscrossing pulsing blue veins. The bulbous crown was throbbing a lusty purple, and the very sight of it made me lick my lips. I grabbed his mighty cock and slowly glided my hands over it a few times, taking it down to the root and circling my fingers around the base. That elicited a low, steady moan from Bart and he whispered hoarsely, "Suck it, man." His cock felt hot inside my paw, and I couldn't wait to get my mouth on it. "Suck it," he said again. I was only too happy to oblige the stud, so I kneeled before him and started to swallow his meat until it was banging against the back of my throat. I corkscrewed my head over and over again, lovingly working on his meat until Bart's moans got louder and louder and I knew I was doing a great job of sucking his dick.

As I continued sucking, my head bobbing wildly over his throbbing piece, I was inspired to explore his inviting ass and see what kind of reaction I'd get. I slowly moved my hands to his furry buttocks and slipped a finger into his crack. His asshole felt hot and slick, and since Bart had made no protest I continued farther, sticking my finger in deeper and deeper until he responded with a long, deep moan of supreme macho pleasure that warmed the cockles of my heart. "God, oh, god," he kept on saying as I massaged his hole with my finger until he cried out and turned around and pushed backward, offering his ass to me. "Suck my ass," he cried. "Stick your fuckin' tongue up my asshole!"

I was only too anxious to do as he wanted, so I stuck my tongue out and landed it right on his puckers, fluttering them to and fro until another loud moan of pleasure escaped his lips.

"Oh, yeah, yeah! That tongue feels good in there, man, hmm. More, man. More!" He was rubbing the nipples that capped his heaving pecs. "Eat my ass, goddamn it!" he suddenly screamed, beating his chest with his fists like an angry gorilla. Fuck! He really loved my iron-stiff tongue digging into his hole. He was pushing his ass on my face, suffocating me, while I drove deeper into his spasming butthole.

Suddenly he leaped off the ladder, smashed into me and sent us crashing to the ground. Then he grabbed me and kissed me hard, his thick tongue slobbering and digging into my mouth. I was gasping for air, suffocated by his brutal lips. I quickly shimmied out of my jeans and briefs. Instinctively, I lifted my legs and circled them around his waist, my calves resting on his beefy thighs. He quickly mounted me, his hairy nipples digging into mine, my fat nut sac pressed against his as he moved forward to plunge his grade-A piece of meat up my ass. My eyes were fixed on his handsome face as he pressed his hairy knees around me, and the reality of being fucked by this big, brawny stud was starting to set in. As his balls collided with mine, I flashed back to earlier when I had noticed how his balls were hanging low inside his hairy nut sac. I recalled how big they'd looked, filled with bull-sperm, sperm that he was going to shoot up my ass! Yeah, I bet that load had been building up ever since he got out of prison.

Service him, that's what I had to do. Take care of my man! This ex-con bull-stud! I looked deep into his eyes, and it was as if I could read his mind. He was going to plow me good, nonstop. Ride my ass. I could see it beginning to break out on his forehead, rich, stinking sweat. "Oh, yeah," he began to moan, getting into the fuck now, moving his hips a bit from side to side as he worked his fat cock in and out of my hole. I could feel his fucking hot heat emanating from his body.

He was just looking at me, staring deep into my eyes as if he were transmitting messages to my mind. He was telling me what he wanted. He wanted his cock deep up my hole; he wanted to suffocate me with his bulk.

Yes, he was thinking all of this as he drove his cock deeper and deeper into my ass. He was a hulking brute and relentless. My hands were on his butt, one firmly clamped on each asscheek, pulling him into me so that he could plow deeper and more furiously. My tight, twitching anal ring was clutching his cock like a man struggling for air.

I brought my knees around his thighs, hunching up a bit, further offering him my ass. He responded by sneering and snarling, his face fierce and angry, simply proud of his huge meat, proud of the man-load that he was going to squirt up my hole. Beads of sweat were breaking out on his forehead and running down, soaking his heavy eyebrows and making them glisten. He was glaring at me now, his black eyes filled with lust and power. We were both being carried away by the excitement we had aroused in each other.

Bart's hefty balls went on banging against my sac as this horny, furry stud gave me one hell of a pounding! The air was pierced with my cries and whoops of delight and his own lusty grunts as he pumped, both of us caught up in a wild, erotic frenzy.

"Unnngh, unnngh, unnngh," he grunted wildly, plowing and plunging away as I grabbed his shoulders and then his neck for support, hoisting myself up and over his cock, which he sank inside me over and over again with long, brutal thrusts, riding me hard for a good half hour. My hands clutched his glutes during this wild bronco ride as he thrust harder and deeper and deeper still until he exploded inside me, the torrents of his cum splashing and burning my aching asshole, his mouth grinding on mine, his lips squashing my moans and groans of ecstasy as I unleashed my own load against his furry, sweat-soaked belly.

When the lusty spasms shaking his muscles had subsided, he lay on top of me, trapping me with his sweat-soaked bulk and panting hard. We found ourselves kissing each other again, long moans punctuating the sounds of sloppy wet kisses. He hunched down a bit and sniffed my armpits, taking in a few musk-fragrant blasts through his sensual nostrils and then tracing down a trail of spit as he licked my chest, abs and crotch, inhaling the deep, rich odor of my short and curlies now drenched with pungent sweat and salty cum. He began licking my groin, lapping up at the spooge that lay nestled in my dark pubic hairs.

Suddenly, he got up. "Fuck, I need a beer!" He went into the house and came back with a six-pack and handed me a beer. "Yeah, I really like the feel of my cock up your asshole. Good and tight," he added, patting my knee with his paw. He grinned for a moment. "Especially when I really get it deep up your hole!" I grabbed his heavy hung cock again, my hand curling around the immense shaft, just waiting for it to get hard so he could fuck me again. He was going to ride me hard, again and again. Yeah, Bart certainly had proved once and for all that things are bigger and better in Texas.

# THRESHER

Elazarus Wills

They appeared on the prairies of western Kansas like beautiful dreams every autumn—the contract wheat-threshing crews peopled mostly with young men from farms across four or five states: Kansas, Nebraska, Iowa, Oklahoma (especially Oklahoma) and eastern Colorado. Felix was from southern Oklahoma, the pan and not the handle. Felix the beautiful. Felix the god. *Felix.*

Felix was the youngest of four sons of Mexican parents, descendents of Mayans and Spaniards, who had emigrated north in the 1980s and who, with their family, had spent their lives moving from one large cattle ranch to another as the market, the owners and the levels of their skills changed. As the boys grew older and even more bronzed in western sun, the elder joined his father in working the cattle and the constant repairing of windmills, fences and aging farm equipment. Then, eventually, the eldest moved off to work at a neighboring or distant ranch—and so it was with the next brother and the next, on down to Felix.

At the age of nineteen Felix was the most beautiful, valuable and talented thing on his Oklahoma ranch home, the modern West equivalent of a Southern plantation. The land and cattle were owned by a Japanese corporation and worked by mostly Texicanos with a smattering of paler out-of-work oil field workers. The foreman was a leather-tough sixty-year-old who had lost his own family ranch in Nebraska to the bottle decades before but now saw through clearer eyes than most, and he saw Felix for the treasure he was—a true, born mechanic in a land of know-it-all tinkerers. He had looked past the wide brown eyes, curly black hair and white teeth contrasting with chocolate brown skin and seen a machine—a brilliant living machine who understood other machines the way that the foreman understood cattle or the vagaries of the Oklahoma and Texas weather.

Felix, from an early age, had watched the alcoholic older men, who shaved only every third day, take engines apart and reassemble them while singing old Merle Haggard songs off-key, staving off the inevitable effects of entropy for a few hundred more hours, sometimes more or sometimes much less. Then he began to help, learn and finally to dominate. The old men would sit in the shade of machine sheds or on the north side running boards of hay trucks, smoking hand-rolled cigarettes and sipping at jars of lemonade laced with tequila, watching in amazement as the brown teenage boy, pretty as a girl but with muscles like a man, took a diesel engine apart, rethreaded dying bolts and deciphered the secret lives of malfunctioning carburetors and fuel injectors with obvious and intuitive joy. Men sometimes gave Felix their best tools out of a sense of admiration under the influence of alcohol.

By the time Casey Neill met him he was almost a decade older, had a truck outfitted as a rolling garage machine shop and was traveling with the best of the threshing crews where a good mechanic was worth his weight in rubies, a world all about large roaring machines moving day and night. *And men.*

Casey was nothing much, tall, skinny, the only son of a small-town newspaper publisher, humoring his father by earning money in the wheat fields around Mazur County during threshing season. He couldn't do many of the jobs, being different, lacking many of the masculine social skills that much of the group-coordinated farmwork required, but he could drive a truck from the fields to the grain elevators in town, an eight-hour shift, a few hours' sleep on a pickup seat and then back at it. He had done it for three seasons and had begun what was to be his last before leaving for California and college, when he met Felix.

He had experienced crushes before directed at other workers; how could he be around naked-to-the-waist, chaff-speckled male flesh and not be attracted, sometimes even madly obsessed? It had been the main reason he agreed to do the mostly disagreeable job each season, looked forward to it even. *Men.* Men, mostly young, tanned and innocent of such things as worrying about skin cancer, with lean bodies that for these few years would function as well as they ever would. Athletes of the fields. Then there was Felix.

Felix was twenty-eight, older than most of the workers and unique in that he traveled *with* them but remained alone. Casey first met him when his unloaded grain truck had broken down on a return trip from the wheat elevators in Mazurton. After a radio call to the foreman, Felix had arrived in less than fifteen minutes, wearing denim jeans pulled down over black high-top boots and a black-on-yellow T-shirt that said: God, Guns and Oil—Welcome to Oklahoma, featuring a derrick with an American flag on top. The shirt was old and faded with a scattering of tiny holes in the fabric stretched across Felix's torso.

"Buenos," Felix had said and listened as Casey described the symptoms of the three-decade-old truck before it had belched black smoke and coasted to a stop. Felix listened to Casey's recounting of mechanical symptoms with closed eyes and then set to work beneath the hood. From time to time his dark head would appear, eyes bright, with a widening line of a smile, and Casey could feel this god's eyes linger on his naked torso, shiny with sunscreen rather than honest sweat.

The repair, which would have taken a normal garage the better part of a day, took all of half an hour with Felix running an air hose from a compressor on his truck to power many of his tools. He stood balanced on the front pipe grill of the truck and leaned down into the engine like a dancer holding a pose. He moved from there to the running board of the old International and from one side to the other. At one point he removed his own shirt, exposing a smooth, hairless chest, with an arrow of dark curls ascending from waist to just above his snug, well-formed navel. A small golden cross, suspended on a chain of the same color, encircled his neck, swinging free as he leaned over the engine.

Showers of sparks from a small air-powered grinder flew and wordless declarations of what sounded like joy emerged from within the shadow of the alligator jaw of the hood. Casey tried to watch what was happening while trying not to be in Felix's pathway in his quick dashes to his garage-truck for a tool or just making a rapid, catlike change of position. At times Felix seemed to be entirely unaware of Casey and would have run over or through him had he not moved aside quickly enough.

Once, Felix had placed a hand on Casey's bare shoulder moving past him. The palm was rough and cool. Casey's semi-erection hardened and as he pressed at his jeans to rearrange its position, Felix's head turned from his work and eyes met eyes and moved downward. The mechanic's smile widened a little, the tip of his tongue emerged and retracted and, after a long beat, he returned his attention to the engine.

Several minutes passed and Casey leaned in closer. Felix was reattaching metal tubing to the carburetor with quick sure motions, holding one section of a fitting in place with one hand tool while tightening it with another. He looked over and smiled several times as he worked. Casey was perched on the opposite fender; head now less than a foot from the mechanic's own, he could smell him, distinct from the aroma of machine. It was a pleasant odor, more plantlike than the sometimes sour, unwashed one that emanated from some of the other thresher boys when Casey passed close by.

The moment, when it came, was liquid. Casey had moved a little closer, one hand gripping the edge of the engine compartment, senses filled with the smell of oily metal and Felix. The mechanic replaced a combination wrench into a labeled pocket of the canvas holder rolled out across the top of the radiator and took up another of a slightly larger size. A half-inch exchanged for a five-sixteenths. The International was a creation of a pre-metric, American-made world.

Then Felix's hand was curving around the back of Casey's neck, pulling him closer—the feel of rough, powerful, blood-filled fingers contrasting with the cool steel of the combination wrench still held in that hand. Their lips met and Casey felt his mouth automatically open against Felix's. The mechanic's tongue entered, writhing and caressing. The taste of Felix's mouth was akin to his earthy smell, something herbal and clean. Casey's own tongue was submissive beneath the intense invasion of Felix's—unfamiliar but delicious.

When Felix finally broke the kiss, the surface of Casey's mind was tinted with hazy want. Felix slid to the ground on his side of the truck and moved around, pausing to restore his wrenches to the canvas holder.

"It is fixed," he said, his accent as smoothly seductive as his body. His hands grasped Casey's hips and, without perceptible effort, he lifted him from the dusty road shoulder to the running board. "Up." Felix was pointing to the rim of the high-sided wooden dump bed and Casey scrambled upward, propelled by Felix's hands under his shoes and by a rising excitement. Casey pulled himself over the edge of the grain box and dropped down to the chaff-covered bed, sneezing from the explosion of fine particles. Felix immediately followed, landing lightly next to him.

The kiss immediately resumed, this time even more forceful, tongue slashing and the mechanic's herbed breath accelerating. Felix's left hand moved between Casey's denim-covered thighs and pressed upward. He grinned in apparent reaction at what he felt while Casey ran his hands over his bare shoulders and down across his chest, pausing to touch the rough links of the gold chain. He tentatively brushed fingertips across the bulge of crotch and was immediately encouraged by Felix's hand pressing down over his.

Casey's entire sexual experience up to that moment, outside of masturbation, had consisted of a less than well-defined *wanting* of boys proceeding to, or interrupted by, early fumblings with a friendly, curious girl, which had seemed more interesting to him than erotically sexual, which was how he felt around the naked, jostling football players after gym class. Or when wrestling. Oh, yes—wrestling with an extra-tight jockstrap and protective cup large enough to conceal his enjoyment. Fun with the boys was one thing—but here was a man, as tall as himself with an extra fifty pounds of muscle and confidence. A man who was now pressing lightly at his naked shoulders—making a clearly communicated physical request.

Casey knelt and worked at Felix's belt. The mechanic did not attempt to help but instead stretched his arms outward and up to grasp the slats of the truck-box sides above his head. Casey got the belt undone, zipper down, fly spread wide, pressing his palm against the vertical extension of erection shrouded beneath blue cotton boxers. He felt dizzy and took several gasping gulps of air to clear his head. He looked up at Felix's face and saw open-mouthed, exposed-teeth desire, an expression that amplified as Casey's fingers, probing through the front underwear flap, touched his cock.

Cock. Felix's cock. It was long, extending from the tip of Casey's central finger to just below the bend in his wrist, thick too—nearly the width of a pair of fingers pressed together. Casey carefully extracted a nearly hairless scrotum, loose in the warmth of the day, through the opening and brought his lips to its surface, which was soft with a slight gooseflesh texture. He gave it a kiss and stroke with his tongue, and the taste was not unpleasant: salt, herb and lust. Holding a portion in his mouth he looked upward again for encouragement and approval, waiting for a hand to descend and grasp his hair, force his mouth to the cock itself, as happened in a certain frequently reoccurring dream. But the mechanic remained as he had been, arms extended as if his wrists were secured in place by iron bands. The contortions of his face against the background of the cobalt sky above and the opening and closing of his jaw, the forward arch of belly and hips, told Casey all that he needed. It was an attitude of domination while suggesting the offering of a sacrifice. *Take me or else...*

Casey heard a vehicle as it approached on the county road, another grain truck with a full load from the sound of it, headed to town. A horn honked and it went on.

*Cock. Felix's cock.* It tasted—of what? Salt? Damp, rich

earth? The air after a prairie storm? Casey took the head into his mouth, tongue traveling over its lower surface, experiencing its taste, texture and a secret, rapid heartbeat throb—the core of this beautiful man. He could feel his own heart throbbing through blood vessels in his neck and behind his eardrums.

He proceeded as best he could with only imagination and the rhythmic thrusts of Felix's hips as a guide. His mind was a blur of desire and his movements felt less than voluntary, slowing and ceasing only after the fluid came, was consumed and Felix was pulling away, a softening cock sliding from between Casey's lips.

"Buenos," Felix whispered in Casey's right ear.

Out of the truck bed, they spoke only a few more words, perfunctory and meaningless. Felix closed and latched the hood before the truck had been restarted, an action that said much that needed to be known about his confidence in his work.

"Tonight, when you rest," was all that Felix said, calling it out in his molasses voice after he had gotten back in his garage truck. *Tonight*. He pulled away and was gone, a flag of Kansas dust rising in his wake, not waiting to confirm his mechanical success. The International roared to life at the first turn of the key in the ignition. Casey was not surprised.


On his last run of the eight-hour shift, Casey used an hour of the four when he could have been sleeping to stop by the house in town to shower and change clothes. It was nearly nine in the evening. His mother, Maya, pale, beautiful and melancholy by nature, was in the kitchen at the table writing something and insisted on heating a plate of leftovers from the earlier dinner.

"You don't look tired," she commented. And he wasn't, even though he needed sleep before he was required back in the fields and on the roads just after midnight. The taste of Felix was still in his mouth. There had been a screed of clouds on the horizon to the southwest all afternoon meaning there would be no letup in the round-the-clock rush to get the grain from the fields to the shelter of the elevators as the crews and machines moved from farm to farm.

As Casey drove, headlights on, back toward the current harvest farm, the air from the open window smelled too clean, sharp and dustless, which he knew meant rain. He drove past the fields where the combines ran in diagonal formations of a half dozen, each about two machine lengths ahead of the next, halogen lights making the area before them nearly bright as day—a temporary sunrise.

The garage truck was parked well away from the illumination of the farmyard, twenty feet from several of the other spare or off-duty grain haulers. Casey shut off his lights before pulling in next to Felix's truck, got out and tapped tentatively at the passenger-side door glass. After a moment there came the sound of the door being unlatched from the inside and Casey climbed inside.

It was a good-sized vehicle, converted from a four-wheel-drive fire truck built for rough country, with the original second set of seats behind the first removed to make a sleeping compartment. Casey could see all of this in the glow of a small mounted television: the truck cab and sleeper bed, plus a naked Felix.

"Welcome," Felix said from the shadows as a hand patted at the quilt-covered mattress. Casey climbed between the backs of the front seats into the space and was immediately seized and pulled into a kiss, a kiss that felt passionate but lasted less than a half minute before the hands pressed at his shoulders—and he complied.

The rain when it arrived at midmorning on the next day was brief, and combines paused only for a few hours during the weather and after the sun had returned.

* * *

That became their pattern over the season, Casey servicing Felix
in the garage truck several times a week. Sometimes they talked
a little, Felix, a few words about his childhood and Casey, much
more, about his family and this place. Casey avoided mentioning
until the arrival of the last week he would be with the crew that
he was leaving for California in a few days, but that maybe he
would return the following summer. Saying that, however tentatively, was a surprise to Casey since from the time he had been
fourteen and more clearly aware of the world beyond this place,
his plan had been attached to an imagined arrow that pointed
west with no intention of a return—ever.

It wasn't just the half promise, it was a practical thing, Casey
told himself. Since his scholarship to the University of California
at Berkeley covered only tuition, with the student or student's
family being expected to provide the rest, Casey returned to
Mazur County the following summer to help out with the family
business and to finish out the season with the thresher crew. He
had discarded his previous ideas of a full-time seasonal job in
Berkeley or San Francisco, and in fact had quit the part-time,
evening restaurant job he had taken during the school year.
     Felix was there with his truck as the foreman gave general
instructions on the crew's first day in the county, but the
mechanic didn't greet Casey or even smile in his direction. There
was heavy weather expected the following week so every piece
of equipment would be running. The contract thresher company
was being paid by the acre harvested, and rain meant lost money
for everyone.
     Casey had worked several shifts without seeing a sign of
Felix who had been kept busy, as the older machines, being
pressed back into regular service, had experienced a series of

minor problems. Casey listened to the back and forth chatter over the radio in whichever truck he was driving. Since every truck was kept in motion he slept in barns and sheds on top of platforms formed from bales of straw. On the night of his third day back on the thresher crew, Casey awoke to a hand on his shoulder. It was in the small hours after midnight and there was no light in the barn, but he could smell Felix. It all seemed very much the same as the year before. Almost. There was something that had changed from his memory. Something a little different, a slight sour, metallic edge, but maybe it was just the nature of the remembering itself. He arose and followed him.

In the sleeping cab of Felix's truck the mechanic stripped quickly out of his clothes, although Casey could only *hear* it happen. A sliver of moon hanging tentatively in the western sky diluted the blackness only a little, revealing only gray, vaguely detailed shapes. Felix kissed Casey lightly and almost immediately pressed him downward in the old familiar way. Casey complied while at the same time feeling a certain measure of resistance, of resentment. The year at the university had not been uneventful, and despite the rapidly escalating fear of AIDS and a sense of unease in certain quarters about the nation under Ronald Reagan (more than one professor's lectures had included diatribes detailing the perceived evils of the man), Casey's sexual experience had been greatly broadened. Liberalized. But now, down he went, regardless.

The mechanic was kneeling as well due to the size of the space, naked, thighs apart; spine bowed backward, arms raised and hands pressed into opposite corners of the compartment. It was all familiar and welcome, mostly. Only the change of odor was different, but not unpleasant.

Felix writhed and emitted little cries as Casey took his cock into his mouth, sliding it in and out while caressing the tight cheeks of the older man's ass with both hands, squeezing, massaging and even probing with a finger. A gentle brush of teeth on tight flesh and a flourish with the tip of the tongue under the cap before ascending—lessons learned, applied. Sometimes the motion of the mechanic's hips took over, and Casey allowed his mouth to be penetrated while his head remained still. When the moment arrived and Casey could feel Felix's body tense, he moved to withdraw, intending to complete the act with a saliva-moistened hand, lessening the risk.

Felix preempted the precaution and, ignoring the token physical protest, abandoned his preferred pose, bringing both hands to bear on Casey's head and finishing deep inside his mouth. It took an effort not to spit it out.

"Buenos," Felix said after a while.

The season passed quickly as it always did. Casey sought out Felix in his truck several more times, but found himself resisting the urge much more often. After that first night, Felix had never taken the initiative of approaching him. When he gave in and went to him he tried to assert himself, if only a little, and vary the routine but Felix would have none of it, stopping any variation with a firm, "No." Once Casey tried to undress beyond taking his shirt off and was again halted. All he had managed in improving the situation during the course of half a dozen encounters was to be allowed to take his own cock out and quietly masturbate while the mechanic fucked his mouth. Felix neither encouraged nor discouraged the act of self-pleasure, but he was obviously aware of it and he allowed it.

While riding the bus back to California, Casey met an older man, in his early fifties, long divorced and on his way to visit a daughter. When the bus was delayed in a Nevada town for a few hours waiting for an engine part to arrive (Casey thought of Felix), Casey and Chris locked themselves in a restaurant bathroom. Chris gave him a speedy and efficient blow job, jerking him to orgasm into a carefully positioned wad of toilet paper and thanking him afterward.

"That was nice," Chris said, a little moisture still visible in his carefully trimmed salt-and-pepper beard as they sat drinking coffee and eating ham and green pepper omelets.

"Nice," Casey said, feeing relaxed and a little sleepy after the release. He wished that they could hurry up with the repairs on the bus. He wished he could ask Chris to sit somewhere else once they had reboarded.

The summer of his sophomore and junior years were spent back in Kansas in the same pattern of routine: working for his dour, uncommunicative father; listening to his beautiful, unhappy mother whisper late-night confessions about how this uninspiring prairie town had imprisoned and crushed her soul—and, once the threshing crew arrived in Mazur County, having less-than-frequent one-sided sex with Felix the gorgeous and brilliant mechanic.

At some point during the third summer Casey began to study Felix beyond just being the most attractive man he had ever seen. He tried to sequester his own emotions and observe Felix as a stranger might, a stranger with no sexual interest in him.

Felix lived a very ordered and self-controlled life. He did not socialize with anyone in the crew and spent almost all of his waking hours working on machines or cleaning, maintaining and repairing his own tools. Felix did not drink, take drugs, read books or engage in small talk. Performing an unvarying sex act with Casey appeared to be his only direct human contact, otherwise he was summoned to fix broken machines, and with machines lay his true affinity. He loved machines. He *lived* machines and Casey Neill was probably seen as a machine, or tool, with a single useful function. Or so Casey gradually began to realize and reaching this conclusion he disposed of any expectations he might have had for Felix. In the times that they were together he performed the function that Felix expected, providing a sexual release to this otherwise mechanical man, but it became a technical exercise for him. In and out in five minutes. Task performed. He found that Felix appreciated increased efficiency.

"Buenos. Muy buenos," Felix would say and go and open the truck door, sending him back into the night.

The next year Casey returned to Mazurton with his new journalism degree and a newspaper job waiting for him in Kansas City. This time his goal was to produce a feature article about the migrant threshing crews, something he could use to further his career. His mother, Maya, was as desperately unhappy as ever, his father as taciturn. Maya wore her unhappy resentment like an outsized diamond provided by her husband. Both expressed satisfaction at the accomplishment of their only son who was now officially educated and launched upon the seas of the world while they huddled on the shore.

Casey continued his observations, in his writing editing out his personal knowledge of Felix, but highlighting his importance in the scheme of the wheat harvest. Felix the man, who loved tools and machines, people not so much. He made a pact with himself to avoid intimacy with Felix this final summer, not go to him no matter how strong the pull. He had just broken from a three-year relationship at Berkeley, his lover leaving to take a yearlong fellowship in Japan and he departing to his low-level staff writer job on a KC daily, by way of Mazur County, Kansas.

It was 10:00 p.m. on a rainy Tuesday night, several days

before the harvest end. The machines were silent in the fields, and the men and boys were mostly asleep or at the Storm Shelter Tavern in town, waiting for the sky to clear and sunshine to dry the grain. Casey tapped on the glass on the passenger-side window of the garage truck. He could hear noises from within— probably Felix's television. He rapped again, a little louder this time. More sounds, definitely not the television. The door opened wide enough for Felix's face to appear. He looked unhappy.

"Tomorrow," Felix said. Then behind him something moved. Casey, acting on pure instinct, yanked the door handle toward him, and a naked Felix came tumbling out onto the gravel. A brown-haired girl, someone from town, appeared under the dome light in the cab. She was brushing at her lips with the back of her hand.

"Felix?" she said.

Felix got up and climbed back into the truck. "Tomorrow," he said again as he shut the door on himself and his new tool.

"Not tomorrow," Casey said to himself.

The day after that it stopped raining in the early morning, after breakfast, and the crews were moving again by midafternoon. The day after that the wheat from Mazur County was all in the concrete silos next the railroad tracks, and Casey Neill was driving north on the state road to get to the Interstate, then east to Kansas City. He was singing aloud with something on the radio and looking forward to tomorrow and the days after.

He would not return for the harvest the following summer.

# BLACK CAULK

## Zeke Mangold

If you dip your balls into it, this could be like the Hollywood Walk of Fame," said the chew-sucking construction worker from behind a killer pair of Oakleys.

In keeping with his clumsy reputation, Dell had stepped into a wet patch of cement in the middle of what was to be L'Affaire, a French fine-dining venue at the third-tier hotel-casino where he worked. Dell disliked French cuisine because it brought to mind images of frog legs, snails, and cheesy soups with too many onions.

"Just my nuts?" said Dell, being a good sport. "Hollywood, here I come."

Dell's career in the food and beverage department of Baja Palace Gambling Hall & Oasis had ended with a whimper rather than a bang. Despite showing up for work every single day, he did little to impress his supervisors. He watched in horror as his deformed, brown-nosing colleagues ascended from the position of bar back to bartender and finally to assistant manager, in a matter of a few months. Seeing no chance for promotion, he reenrolled at the University of Nevada, Las Vegas, this time majoring in hospitality. He also applied for an internship in Baja Palace's human resources department and, having given a service training manager there an uncharacteristically positive feeling, Dell found himself working in a cubicle, wearing a tie and surfing the corporate-provided Internet every morning before leaving to attend afternoon classes. His mother, a UNLV sociology professor, seemed quite proud; even she loathed big gaming corporations for their amoral capitalism and anti-union practices.

In any case, it was expected that Dell would create, from scratch no less, original PowerPoint presentations of training modules wherein new hires would learn about Baja Palace's unique service culture. Like any college student worth his bongwater, Dell had Googled the term "unique service culture" and acquired just what he needed: an entire semester's worth of student presentations that a goofy Kentucky college professor had posted on his class website, where anyone could simply download the material and replace company names with, say, "Baja Palace." In other words, Dell had completed six months of work in three hours' time. Which meant, when he wasn't trying to look busy, he had lots of time to kill.

So he wandered Baja Palace. One morning Dell decided to walk off a particularly bad breakfast courtesy of the employee dining room by checking on the progress of the new Parisian eatery being installed on the property's west side, where the RV park had once stood. Like every other hotel-casino in Vegas, Baja Palace sought to elevate its brand by teaming up with a celebrity chef to create a luxury product for the moneyed and elite. If this kept up, Dell supposed, an off-Strip joint on Boulder Highway like Baja Palace would soon be off-limits to people making less than a million dollars annually. The notion didn't bother him, of course. Unlike his liberal, good-hearted mother, Dell despised the poor.

Which is why he felt confused when suffering extreme arousal at the sight of a scrawny construction worker bent over in a door frame and wielding a caulking gun, his tight, pale cheeks peeking out from a tighter pair of Levi's 501s. He wore a do-rag, but in a sexy way. Blue-collar people were usually ugly and smelled bad. Not this ripped specimen, who emitted a phero-mone so tasty Dell knew he'd have to spank off later in the HR restroom, something he only did in extreme situations.

"Hollywood folk ain't got no balls," cracked the construc-tion worker who resembled a young Brad Pitt, only with genuine white trash credentials. "That's why them liberals press their hands in there instead, see. They're too busy braiding their hippie vagina hair and feeling sorry for terrorists to put their nuts on the line for anything."

"Christ, are you serious?" said Dell.

"Hah! Hell, no. I just enjoy saying terrible things."

"I can relate. Hey, is your freedom restaurant making any progress?" Having left his shades in the office, Dell tried not to stare at the yummy tattoos on the man's slender, sweat-drenched arms.

"Oh, I get it. Yeah, freedom will ring here shortly, my friend." The construction worker spit into a paint bucket before extending his hand. "Name's Wayne."

Dell shook, felt rough calluses. He longed to be manhandled by this brute. "Dell. That's good, Wayne. Can't beat the taste of snails and frog legs, I'm telling you."

"I'll take your word for it. Speaking of French, I love those *Transporter* movies with that French guy, what's-his-face? Looking forward to seeing the new one."

"Jason Statham. Actually, he's British."

"Is he now."

"Love those movies. Yes, but he speaks French, too."

"Figures," said Wayne, grinning.

*God, his lips are succulent morsels,* thought Dell. He wanted Wayne to spit char juice—and other fluids—into his mouth. Moreover, Dell's gay spider sense was tingling. This dude was talking way too much to be straight and narrow, his body language far too relaxed. Time to test the waters.

"You know, I work in HR, so I have movie passes for casino employees. How about we hit Regal Cinemas after work? There's a five fifteen screening of *Transporter II.*"

"Huh," said Wayne, pondering it. He pointed the caulking gun to his temple and gazed up at the blue sky.

"Come on," insisted Dell. "I'm here to put the free in freedom."

"Hah! Sure, I'll see you at the theater at, like, five."

Dell had to bite his lip to keep from dancing his way back to work. As soon he sat down in his cube, he loaded a Goldfrapp DVD onto his computer and called his best friend, London.

The two of them reclined in comfy leather chairs at Dragon Nails, reading old issues of *Star* and allowing SARS-masked Asian women to administer pedicures. In an effort to get in touch with her heritage, London was spending more and more time in the Las Vegas Chinatown, basically a few blocks of strip malls loaded with grocers, sushi joints, massage parlors and fish markets. She knew nothing of these businesses, of course, and her idea of "re-immersion" involved paying for a fake tan inside an Asian-owned salon. London wasn't impressed with Dell's majoring in hospitality, his internship or his potential boyfriend.

"Working in an office makes your dick soft," she warned him.

She seemed confident that she and Dell were the only English-speaking people in the salon. "Turns you into a eunuch. I know this because I get paid to quote-end quote 'fuck' these business admin types. They rarely get it up. In the end, they're just paying for very intense lap dances."

This was true. After a year of seriously working the pole, London graduated to the arena of high-end hooking, coordinating her illegal trade with bartenders at a few of the hottest nightclubs on the Strip. An increasing number of corporate suits flooded Vegas, and London serviced as many as she could during the few nights she was on call. Making five thousand dollars per john, she lived in the ritzier part of Summerlin and drove not one but two BMWs. She adored German machinery.

Dell shrugged. "I'll take Viagra if it gets that bad."

"It doesn't work as well as you think. Besides, you're definitely not the top in that relationship."

"What do you mean?"

"Wayne is a construction worker. He pitches but doesn't catch."

"I'll make him catch."

London looked at Dell, sunglasses sliding to the tip of her nose. "He'll catch the clap is what."

To their surprise, the pedicurist handling Dell's feet paused for a moment to observe his reaction, which made the hospitality major laugh.

"There's only one clap-infected prostitute in this salon," Dell announced.

London swatted him with a rolled-up *Star*.

Dell skipped class, his first that semester. Then again, he was only two weeks in. They met in front of the theater at five. Hair slicked, Wayne had obviously showered somewhere and changed into jeans and a black T-shirt. He still wore his boots, though.

"Nice," said Dell. "Where'd you find a shower?"

"Locker rooms," Wayne said with a smirk. Sunglasses off and hanging from his shirt collar, Wayne had hazel eyes. Dell thought they were lovely.

"You eat in the employee dining room?"

Wayne frowned. "So what. Going to rat on me?"

"No. Getting the shits is punishment enough."

"Hah!"

Using Dell's passes, they chatted while threading their way toward the concession stand. Dell learned a bit about Wayne. Originally from Bakersfield, he'd been married once and had moved to Vegas because of the construction boom. Then, at one point, he "joked" about the many truck-stop glory holes between here and Barstow.

It was music to Dell's ears.

Wayne selected seats in the very last row. To Dell's relief, the theater wasn't crowded; the closest patrons were nearly a dozen aisles away. The lights dimmed. Dell and Wayne watched the trailers quietly and, for the first ten minutes, their eyes remained glued to the screen as violent mayhem surged ever onward.

And then Wayne quietly slipped his hands into Dell's pants and began jerking him off.

Dell removed his tie and unzipped, allowing easier access. When he reached a mighty erection, Wayne went down on him, sucking his prick with smooth yet firm pressure, using his rough fingers to caress Dell's balls. For such an uncultured soul, he gave a velvet blow job. At one point, Wayne stopped sucking in order to tongue Dell's piss slit, causing waves of pleasure to ripple across his spine. The fear of getting caught made him hornier.

"Stick your fingers in me," whispered Dell.

Wayne spit into his left palm and plunged an index finger directly into Dell's sphincter, massaging the prostate. Dell removed his pants completely, raising his legs up so that the construction worker could get to work. While continuing to penetrate Dell, Wayne sucked and sucked.

"Let me taste my ass," said Dell. He had douched earlier in the afternoon inside a restroom stall in the HR building.

Wayne inserted his finger past Dell's lips. They tasted a little salty from the saline.

It was too much. Dell exploded in Wayne's mouth. Wayne swallowed dutifully, even as thick cum oozed its way down Dell's shaft. Wayne licked eagerly at that, too.

By now, Dell had already begun stroking Wayne's enormous uncircumcised cock. He was breathing heavy, so Dell went down on him, flicking his tongue underneath and around the soft, musky foreskin.

When he did this, Wayne instantly ejaculated, emitting a tiny whimper with each spurt of boiling semen. Only some of it landed on Dell's tongue, but Wayne's jizz tasted good and funky. Dell wanted more.

There was so much cum on the floor Dell dumped his popcorn on it in order to somehow disguise the mess. While the credits rolled, they exited the theater. Dell noticed that Wayne had donned his Oakleys again. He mumbled something about running late for...wait; did he just say "an Alcoholics Anonymous meeting"? And then he brusquely abandoned Dell, whose heart sank, to stand by himself in the lobby as other movies began to break. Before he could muster the courage to pursue Wayne, people began swirling out, bumping into each other and him.

He didn't know what else to do but call London.

* * *

They met in an obscure North Las Vegas dive bar that, according to a Vegas weekly paper, specialized in jazz. To Dell's irritation, the jazz was smooth.

"This bitch is singing Paul Anka," he said, seething.

The bitch was a wannabe torch singer wearing a red dress that was a tad too small for her hulking frame. She seemed to have burned her hair in the process of a self-administered perm. She had great difficulty singing in tune.

"Gets her fashion cues from Jessica Rabbit," Dell added.

"Sorry he hurt you." London filled Dell's empty glass with Miller Lite and lit herself a menthol Marlboro.

"He's ashamed, I figure."

"Maybe being gay is what he's ashamed of."

"Okay, I don't know him well or at all, sure. Still, I've never had a good-looking guy, like, *sprint* away. It's almost as if, once we stepped out of the darkness, he looked at me again and thought I was hideous."

"You're not hideous. You're a hot college stud."

"It's damaging to the ego, I guess."

"Sure it is."

"And I'm angry at myself."

"What for?"

"I want to see him again. I want him to stay with me overnight."

"At your mom's?"

"No. I don't know. Maybe we could go back to his trailer."

"Surrounded by pit bulls."

"Rusted-out car on blocks."

"Sounds romantic. So why don't you visit your redneck friend at work?"

Dell said nothing. He flinched as the vocalist warbled toward the conclusion of "Lucy in the Sky with Diamonds."

"What would you like to hear?" the singer asked the minuscule audience.

"The door closing behind you," replied Dell.

The singer looked at him blankly. "I don't know that one," she said, before launching into a Celine Dion number, inflicting revenge.

London couldn't stop laughing.

Dell walked past the busy construction site and spotted Wayne, who signaled to the cubical dweller that it was okay to approach. Wayne wore a hard hat this time instead of a bandana. Smiling, he gave Dell a manly hug.

"Sorry I ran out on you," said Wayne. "I'm in AA and really can't miss a meeting. After getting in the car, it dawned on me: I ain't got your number."

"No problem."

"What're you doing tonight?"

Dell shrugged. "Nothing."

"You eat Thai?"

"Boys."

"What?"

"Joke."

"Oh, got it. Hah!"

"What's that?" said Dell, indicating Wayne's caulking instrument.

"It's my black caulk."

"Huh?"

"This French café—L'Fart or whatever—is doing everything in black. Black tile. Black marble. Everything."

"You enjoy black caulk?" Dell joked.

Wayne grinned. "I know about black caulk."

Dell let it go without comment.

That night they dined at Vegas's best Thai joint in Commercial Center, an old strip mall that also housed a gay leather cowboy bar called the Saloon, which drew a black crowd. Dell considered asking Wayne if he'd ever visited the Saloon but thought better of it, given his AA membership.

"Go ahead and order a beer if you want," said Wayne after a waiter set glasses of ice water on the table. He scanned the menu with obvious glee.

"I'm good."

"It won't bother me."

"How long have you been, ah, straight?"

Wayne snickered. "Three years. But by drinking too much, I had developed a pretty decent meth habit. Drinking led me into a lot of nasty corners that I was lucky enough to escape from. It's amazing I'm still alive."

They dined on grilled catfish and deep-fried beef jerky, and remained content with ice water. Wayne ended up revealing a lot about himself over dinner. For his part, Dell talked very little but listened intently. He wanted Wayne to feel comfortable.

And then the construction worker brought up black caulk.

"So are you ready?"

"For what?"

"Hot blackness."

Confusion gripped Dell's brain. "Look, I like toys as much as anyone, but—"

"No, I mean the real thing. Let's go."

Wayne paid the surprisingly affordable check, and the two of them headed to the Saloon. Dell was nervous, as it had been a while since his last visit there. Upon pushing open the swinging doors, though, he felt more at ease. Nothing had changed, except that he was now in here with a lily white construction worker.

Wayne led him into a back room where two black guys were shooting a game of pool. Both wore cowboy hats and boots. One sported a black T-shirt that read: GOT LUBE? They stopped the game to look Dell up and down, as if examining a piece of merchandise. Then they directed their attention to Wayne, waiting for something to happen.

They didn't wait long. Wayne grabbed Dell and kissed him hard on the mouth. Dell reciprocated as Wayne unbuttoned Dell's Diesel jeans and pulled out his schlong. Wayne got right down on his knees and wrapped his lips around Dell's pulsing cock.

The taller black dude left his cue on the table, walked over to Dell and Wayne and whipped out his own meat. "Mind if I join?" Clearly, Wayne had experienced this kind of encounter before or something very similar to it.

Intimidated, Dell didn't say anything. Wayne simply redirected his suction, while still massaging Dell's balls without missing a stroke. Watching Wayne scarf dark meat made Dell horny, the head of his cock becoming engorged, his balls filling with semen. He wanted to cum in Wayne's hot mouth.

Sensing Dell's eagerness, Wayne said, "I'm gonna eat this guy's cum first."

With that, the black guy grabbed Wayne by his ears and began pumping. Wayne gagged a few times but managed to keep up with the vigorous thrusts. Seconds later, the black man ejaculated, his spunk shooting so furiously it spilled out of the construction worker's mouth. Strands of saliva mixed with spunk trailed from Wayne's chin.

"More," he groaned, wiping cum from his lips.

The smaller black guy had already stepped up, his eight-inch cock standing at full mast. Wayne pounced on it. Putting his hand on the top of Wayne's forehead, the black guy carefully guided himself in and out, slowly skull-fucking him.

"Oh, yeah," said the black guy, quickly unloading right into Wayne's hot mouth.

Dell couldn't stand it anymore. He raised Wayne by his arms, bending him over a pool table. Wayne obliged. Dell ripped Wayne's jeans down to his ankles and grabbed a small plastic bottle of lube from atop a cigarette machine, squirting some into his hand.

"I'm going to drill your ass, Wayne."

Wayne was on his side now, with Dell upright behind him at the edge of the pool table. Wayne opened his legs wide, allowing for balls-deep thrusting. Dell held up one of Wayne's legs, continuing to pound the construction worker's tight bunghole. With his other hand, he gave Wayne a solid stroking until he erupted, his hot cum flowing over Dell's hand.

"Ooh," said Wayne.

Suddenly, the first black guy was now back inside Wayne's mouth. Dell watched Wayne suck a big black cock until he felt he was ready to explode.

"All right," said Dell, pulling his cock out of Wayne's ass. "Time to eat cum."

Wayne turned and got down on his knees. He stuck his tongue out, and Dell jerked a huge load right onto it.

"That was tasty," said Wayne.

After Wayne sucked every drop of cum from Dell's dick, the black guys and a few of their friends approached, eager to splatter the construction worker's face.

Balls drained, Dell stepped out into the warm desert air. He left Wayne kneeling in the back room of the Saloon with a cock-stuffed face. For a moment, Dell worried that he and Wayne were victims of their own respective lusts. Or maybe he just needed coffee. He walked through Commercial Center in search of a café.

* * *

London was blowing up his cell. Dell wanted badly to chat with her while sitting at Pride, a GLBT coffee shop that also sold edible underwear. Afterward, he could return to the Saloon to pick up Wayne. He sipped his latté and answered the call.

"You were right," he said. "Construction workers fuck like champs."

"Drop out of college, like, now," said London.

"Right on. But hey, you were wrong about him not catching. Jesus, does he catch."

"Where did you take him? Someplace nice, I hope."

"The Saloon."

"The cowboy dive? Dell!"

"Low class, sure. And you know what? I'm beginning to love it."

# A MARRIED CONSTRUCTION WORKER'S WARM MOUTH

Shane Allison

My dick kicked in my jeans beneath the steering wheel as I sat at the light, PJ Harvey blaring from the speakers. The light took forever to turn. Try Our New Asian Salad, read the McDonald's sign from across the street. It wasn't salad I was hungry for. I just had to get my dick sucked. Beatin' off only goes so far, you know? I pulled into the lot and parked between a Monte Carlo and a Silverado. I hadn't been out here in two weeks. I didn't want to run into that asshole I came to blows with the last time I was here. We walked away with scratches, me with a pair of broken glasses. It could have been a lot worse: son of a bitch could've shot me; the two of us could have ended up in the emergency room with gunshots in our guts just 'cause I wouldn't suck his dick.

I'm scared about coming here during the day, scared that someone's gonna spot me in this bible-beating town, this capital city of Southern Baptists. But I got my needs, you know?

The bell above the door chimed as I walked in. There was

no one behind the counter. I heard girlish giggles. The cashier didn't bother to check and see me. For all she knew, I could've been a curious twelve-year-old. I ducked into the arcade. The place smelled of semen. There was one other guy standing around, studying gay porn with titles like *Slurpin' Jizz, Black Nutz Juice* and *Black and White Twinks in Lust* encased behind locked, plate glass. It was Powder. I got nicknames for them all. I crown him this 'cause he's pale and bald, resembling Sean Patrick Flanery from the movie of the same name. He's everywhere milling around here for men. I sucked his dick once. It was nothing special. I cruised down the hall under the gentle lighting strung high over shadows that reeked of poppers, searching for others that were out looking for afternoon pleasure. Booth three was occupied. I jiggled the knob only to find that it was locked. A cold glow seeped from the slit beneath the door. Booth six was cracked just enough for me to watch some construction-worker type jacking off to straight porn. His dick wasn't much, but still suckable. When I moved in to get a better view, he looked to me like I was a stranger he had never seen before, but never missed a *beat,* so to speak, as he shut himself inside, but I didn't give a shit, 'cause there was someone in booth nine, which is infamous for its glory hole action. These are the nastier stalls of the arcade, with spit and cum in pools and glazing the walls, little whore holes that reek of piss and shit, no one booth ever smelling worse than another.

I crept into nine, which had no doorknob. Most of them are shot to shit like this. Some don't lock while others are equipped with bad machines that steal your money. They say this place is owned by the Russian mafia. I believe it.

I shut myself in and peeked through the hole. It was an older dude, well-dressed in black slacks and a white dress shirt. His dick wasn't out. I took a seat and unzipped, pulled my dick past the copper teeth of my jeans. Didn't take long for things to rise. He stared through gloriously at me, watching me play with my foreskin, diddle my nuts. He summoned me with his fingers and I knew the signal. I pushed my jeans down low, pulled my shirt up out the way and worked my dick through that tennis ball–sized cut out. The booth smelled of ass, but I never did mind the little things. He touched me. His fingers were *pings* of cold. I was tuned to the footsteps outside my stall, one of many that didn't lock, according to the sign.

THIS DOOR IS BROKEN.

THIS BOOTH IS OUT OF ORDER. IF YOU USE THIS BOOTH, IT'S YOUR OWN FAULT WHEN YOU GET STUCK AND NO, WE WON'T HELP YOU OUT WHEN YOU REALIZE YOU'RE STUCK BECAUSE THE BOOTH DOESN'T OPEN.

Someone opened my door, letting out the fornication. It was Powder. He saw that I was busy, up to no good with my ass exposed, dick planted past some old fucker's lips. Powder watched me, which I didn't mind 'cause he's cute. I waved him in to join me, but he just smiled like he does and shut the door, leaving me to my own devices. That geezer's mouth was wet and warm on me. I can't tell you how long it'd been since I'd been blown. The last guy that had me sucked at sucking. He beat my dick up pretty good with those teeth he was giving. He left me scabbed up for days. It was weeks before I could jack off. Had to use the Vaseline for other things.

That silver daddy sucked and slurped, licking dickhead, tongue wrapped around the shaft. Only ten minutes in and I was about to come, but I wasn't ready yet. There was more fun to be had, and I was getting bored with this man's mouth. I pulled out. The dirty bastard lapped at the glory hole, hungry for more of me. I made myself decent. I wanted a new stud muffin. I wanted that dusty stranger closed off from me in booth three. I pressed my ear to his door to listen in on fake screams from porn bitches begging for it.

*Ah, yeah, this* and *Fuck my ass that.* Powder lingered in the dark, watching me. He must have thought me such a slut, but I didn't care because behind these walls of caked-on cum, I'm a dick-sucking whore and I don't care who knows. I jiggled his doorknob again. His pants were down this time, shirt up over that potbelly overgrown with black fur. His dick was thicker. He looked up at me and this time waved me in. I stepped over this worker's boots, squeezing into his booth. It smelled of dirt and sweat. I plucked out my dick, damn near soaked with spit from that silver daddy. Porn-star pussy gleamed in our eyes. We took things slow. I veered my candy toward his mug. The adult actress getting her *phat* black ass pounded turned me on, but not enough.

"Turn it to gay porn," I whispered. He did what I wanted, flipping the channels with his one free hand.

"That's good," I told him. He stopped at a scene of a marine getting butt-fucked by a dirty blond in army garb. I couldn't get any hornier than I was that afternoon. Dicks slithering in and out of the tan-lined asses of hung, Hungarian boys has always been my forte.

"Suck me," I told him. I wanted to feed this dirty worker. When he turned his hat backward, I knew I was in for it. He took deep whiffs from his bottle of poppers. He offered me some, but I refused. I don't know what they get out of it. The stuff only gives me a headache. He was better at it than the dude across the way. I noticed the biggest wedding band on his hand, those nails lined with grit. It made my heart flutter knowing I had down-low lips around my dick. The arcades are no mystery to these sorts. If I had a dime every time I faced-fucked some wifey's husband, my student loans would be paid in full. I pushed off my sneaks, stepped out of my loose fits. I was naked with a worker's rough mitts on my hips, moustached lips around my stuff.

"More spit," I told him. Construction workers are so nasty. He rolled his mouth around, hand going up and down.

"Wanna fuck me?" he asked.

I usually don't in a place like this, a space this size. It's curtains for us if we're caught according to the signs.

ANYONE SUSPECTED OF DOING ANYTHING OTHER THAN PREVIEWING THE MOVIES (STANDING AROUND, TALKING, SEXUAL ACTIVITIES) WILL BE REPORTED TO THE POLICE AND BANNED.

All that shit about fucking in the booths, going on about health risks and final warnings. I hated it when he stopped blowing me. He turned himself off into the corner of the booth, lifting his shirt cured with sweat, smudged with dirt.

"Fuck me," he said.

"I don't have any rubbers," I told him.

"They sell some up front," he said in his country twang.

"Hol' up." I buckled my soaked dick back into my jeans. I unlocked the door, silver porno glow spilling out into the hall full of men that had gathered outside our booth. That filthy worker locked himself in behind me. I stepped up to the counter eying the fishbowl of condoms, the miniature tubes of lubricant.

"How much are the...?" I pointed. Kim was working, thankfully. She's cool with me. She's got a gay brother.

"They're on the house," she smiled. I took one of each.

"Thanks, babe." Kim knew I was about to get some ass. I returned to the back. That daddy from earlier was gone. Powder was lingering about with the others, waiting for the next piece of arcade trade. I knocked nicely. The worker let me in. He was keeping his dick stiff as he watched some barely legal blonde get fucked on top of a pinball machine. I stepped over him and locked us in. I dropped trou and tore the prophylactic out of the foil and rolled it on. He assumed the position, his ass point-blank. I took the lube and slathered on the stuff, smeared the rest up his blue-collar butt. He took me and led me to his bull's-eye. I slid into him so easily. I held on to his shoulders like reins and pushed, worked his ass like there was no tomorrow. Porn mingled with the sounds he made as I fucked the pimpled ass of some wife's husband. We heard the feet of men rustling outside our door, hungry to get in on our action. The muscles in my thighs started to burn, sweat forming. Who knew fucking could be such hard work? We switched positions. I sat in the chair, he straddled me. I glided back in; the chair squeaked to our weight. My glasses fogged from perspiration. When the movie was up, when his money had run out, he fished more out of the breast pocket of his shirt and slid his hard-earned dough into the mouth of the money slot. The worker switched it back to the regularly scheduled smut. *Fuck me, eat my pussy* it went on.

"Come for me," he said. This carpenter's butt was a dream. I could have sworn the chair was going to snap to the floor. I was ready, drawing to a climax. I clawed at his back, pulled his mane of dirty hair as I pumped semen in the rubber, up his butt. My legs damn near collapsed from under me. He sat up off me and shot off onto the monitor. I rolled the rubber off my dick and dropped it on the floor. He went on about how hot it was, how good I could fuck like I hadn't heard that before. I tucked my sloppy dick back into my pants. We opened the door to a gang of cruisers dispersing into the dimly lit arcade. It had grown late. We went in separate directions out of the parking lot, never exchanging names, remaining the same: anonymous.

# ABOUT THE AUTHORS

**BEARMUFFIN** is a native Californian and lives in San Diego where he prowls the bars, bathhouses and wherever you can find horny studs, in a relentless search for grist for his erotic mill. His stories have been published in many gay magazines and his work has appeared in anthologies from Cleis, Alyson and Starbooks.

**H. L. CHAMPA** has appeared in numerous anthologies including *Tasting Him, Like Magnets We Attract* and *College Boys*. If you prefer your erotica in electronic form, short stories can be found at Clean Sheets and Ravenous Romance. Find her online at heidichampa.blogspot.com.

**HANK EDWARDS's** books include *Fluffers, Inc., A Carnal Cruise* and the novella, *Holed Up*. Dozens of his stories have appeared in gay erotic magazines and anthologies. He lives with his partner of many years outside Detroit. Visit his website at hankedwardsbooks.com.

**A. C. FARO** grew up in Los Angeles, with an eight-year stint in Rome, Italy, where the amazing art, culture, ancient monuments and stunning men all contributed to awakening his passion for writing. Several of his erotic short stories, both gay and straight, have been published in the United States and abroad.

**JEFF FUNK's** stories have appeared in *Dorm Porn 2, Tales of Travelrotica for Gay Men Volume 2, My First Time Volume 5, Ultimate Gay Erotica 2008, Cruise Lines* and *Hard Hats*. He lives in Auburn, Indiana.

**WILLIAM HOLDEN** lives in Cambridge, Massachusetts. His writing career spans more than ten years with over thirty short stories. He has served as fiction editor for *RFD Magazine,* authored five bibliographies on LGBT literature and has written various encyclopedia articles on the history of gay fiction and literature. Visit him at williamholdenonline.com.

**ZEKE MANGOLD** lives, loves and fucks in Las Vegas, Nevada.

**NEIL PLAKCY** is the author of *Mahu, Mahu Surfer, Mahu Fire* and *Mahu Vice,* mystery novels set in Hawaii, as well as the romance novels *Three Wrong Turns in the Desert* and *GayLife. com*. He edited *Paws & Reflect: A Special Bond Between Man and Dog* and the gay erotic anthologies *Hard Hats* and *Surfer Boys.*

**MARVIN RICHMOND** is the nom de sex of a complexly part-nered African American poet and writer. His work has appeared in the *Black Fire* and *Just the Sex* anthologies.

**ROB ROSEN,** author of the widely acclaimed novels, *Sparkle: The Queerest Book You'll Ever Love* and *Divas Las Vegas*, has contributed, to date, to more than one hundred anthologies. Please visit him at therobrosen.com.

**DAVID SALCIDO** is the former publisher of Blue Food and has made his living writing for regional and national entertainment magazines for the past twenty years. As a fiction writer, his credits include various periodicals, websites and the anthologies *Blood Lust: Erotic Vampire Tales* and *Redsine Ten.*

**AARON TRAVIS's** first erotic story appeared in 1979 in *Drummer* magazine. Over the next fifteen years he wrote dozens of short stories, the serialized novel *Slaves of the Empire,* and hundreds of book and video reviews for numerous magazines. His stories have also been translated into Dutch, German and Japanese. His web page is stevensaylor.com/AaronTravis/.

**BOB VICKERY** (bobvickery.com) lives in San Francisco and is a regular contributor to various websites and magazines. He has five collections of stories published: *Skin Deep, Cock Tales, Cocksure, Play Buddies,* and most recently, *Man Jack,* an audiobook of some of his hottest stories.

**ELAZARUS WILLS** is a journalist, used bookstore owner and gay erotica author residing in a mountain valley in Colorado. His work has appeared in many anthologies over the past few years including *Best Gay Romance 2010. Thresher* is a freestanding prequel to *A Deeper Well,* a Kansas-set, gay mystery-romance novel.

**ROB WOLFSHAM** has had stories published in *Best Gay Erotica 2010, Boy Crazy: Coming Out Erotica* and *I Like It Like That: True Stories of Gay Male Desire*. He lives in Lubbock, Texas, and continues to write about guys who cross him. Read his blog at wolfshammy.com.

**LOGAN ZACHARY** is a Minneapolis mystery author whose stories can be found in *Hard Hats, Taken by Force, Boys Caught in the Act, Ride Me Cowboy, Best Gay Erotica 2009, Ultimate Gay Erotica 2009, Surfer Boys, SexTime, Queer Dimensions, Obsessed, College Boys, Teammates* and *Rough Trade*. He can be reached at LoganZachary2002@yahoo.com.

# ABOUT
# THE EDITOR

**SHANE ALLISON** is the proud editor of *Hot Cops: Gay Erotic Stories; Backdraft: Hot Fireman Erotica; College Boys: Gay Erotic Stories* and *Homo Thugs*. He has had stories published in over a dozen anthologies including *Best Black Gay Erotica, Sex by the Book, Best Gay Bondage, Ultimate Gay Erotica, Biker Boys, Making the Hook-Up, Surfer Boys* and four editions of *Best Gay Erotica*. His first volume of poetry, *Slut Machine*, is forthcoming from Rebel Satori Press.

# More Gay Erotic Stories from Shane Allison

**Buy 4 books, Get 1 _FREE_***

**College Boys**
*Gay Erotic Stories*
Edited by Shane Allison

First feelings of lust for another boy, all-night study sessions, the excitement of a student hot for a teacher...is it any wonder that college boys are the objects of fantasy the world over?
ISBN 978-1-57344-399-9 $14.95

---

**Hot Cops**
*Gay Erotic Stories*
Edited by Shane Allison

"From smooth and fit to big and hairy... it's like a downtown locker room where everyone has some sort of badge."—*Bay Area Reporter*
ISBN 978-1-57344-277-0  $14.95

**Backdraft**
*Fireman Erotica*
Edited by Shane Allison

"Seriously: This book is so scorching hot that you should box it with a fire extinguisher and ointment. It will burn more than your fingers." —*Tucson Weekly*
ISBN 978-1-57344-325-8  $14.95

---

# More of the Very Best from Cleis Press

**Best Gay Erotica 2010**
Edited by Richard Labonté
Selected and introduced by Blair Mastbaum
ISBN 978-1-57344-374-6  $15.95

**Best of the Best Gay Erotica 3**
Edited by Richard Labonté
ISBN 978-1-57344-410-1  $14.95

**Skater Boys**
*Gay Erotic Stories*
Edited by Neil Plakcy
ISBN 978-1-57344-401-9  $14.95

**A Sticky End**
*A Mitch Mitchell Mystery*
By James Lear
ISBN 978-1-57344-395-1 $14.95

---

* Free book of equal or lesser value. Shipping and applicable sales tax extra.
Cleis Press • (800) 780-2279 • orders@cleispress.com
www.cleispress.com

Ordering is easy! Call us toll free or fax us to place your MC/VISA order.
You can also mail the order form below with payment to:
Cleis Press, 2246 Sixth St., Berkeley, CA 94710.

## ORDER FORM

| QTY | TITLE | PRICE |
|-----|-------|-------|
| ——— | ——————————————————————— | ——— |
| ——— | ——————————————————————— | ——— |
| ——— | ——————————————————————— | ——— |
| ——— | ——————————————————————— | ——— |
| ——— | ——————————————————————— | ——— |
| ——— | ——————————————————————— | ——— |
| ——— | ——————————————————————— | ——— |

SUBTOTAL ————————

SHIPPING ————————

SALES TAX ————————

TOTAL ————————

Add $3.95 postage/handling for the first book ordered and $1.00 for each additional book. Outside North America, please contact us for shipping rates. California residents add 9.75% sales tax. Payment in U.S. dollars only.

*** Free book of equal or lesser value. Shipping and applicable sales tax extra.**

**Cleis Press • Phone: (800) 780-2279 • Fax: 510-845-8001**
**orders@cleispress.com • www.cleispress.com**
**You'll find more great books on our website**

**Follow us on Twitter @cleispress • Friend/fan us on Facebook**